Nothing could fix the wrongness of what her mom had done.

She walked slowly to the Mustang. It wasn't locked. Her mom always said they didn't have anything worth stealing and, if someone did take something, they must need it pretty bad. She probably only said that because the locks didn't work, but maybe she really did mean the part about someone else needing their stuff. Her mom surprised her sometimes. Not usually in a good way, but sometimes. Ivy got in and sat with her head down, holding her hands together to keep them from shaking.

What she wanted to do: walk out of the parking lot and keep walking forever, walk until she was eighteen years old and could start her own life.

She took a sharp breath and huffed it out, then another.

After a while her mother appeared, and they roared from the lot. Apparently the police were not coming.

OTHER BOOKS YOU MAY ENJOY

The Education
of Ivy Blake

ellen airgood

PUFFIN BOOKS

PUFFIN BOOKS

An imprint of Penguin Random House LLC

375 Hudson Street

New York, New York 10014

First published in the United States of America by Nancy Paulsen Books,
an imprint of Penguin Group (USA) LLC, 2015
Published by Puffin Books, an imprint of Penguin Random House LLC, 2016

THE LIBRARY OF CONGRESS HAS CATALOGED THE NANCY PAULSEN BOOKS EDITION AS FOLLOWS:

Airgood, Ellen, author. The education of Ivy Blake / Ellen Airgood.

p. cm.

Companion book to: Prairie Evers

Summary: When eleven-year-old Ivy Blake leaves the nice farm family where
she has been living in upstate New York and moves back in with her mother, she
is finally forced to face up to the fact that her alcoholic, dysfunctional parent will
never be able to provide her with a stable home—and if she wants to achieve
her dreams, she is going to have to take charge of her own future.

1. Mothers and daughters—Juvenile fiction. 2. Children of alcoholics—Juvenile fiction.
3. Dysfunctional families—New York (State)—Juvenile fiction.
4. New York (State)—Juvenile fiction. [1. Mothers and daughters—Fiction.
2. Alcoholism—Fiction. 3. Family problems—Fiction.
4. Family life—New York (State)—Fiction. 4. New York (State)—Fiction.]
I. Title. P27.A28114Ed 2015 813.6—dc23 [FIC] 2014036182

Puffin Books ISBN 978-0-14-242680-7

Printed in the United States of America
Design by Annie Ericsson

1 3 5 7 9 10 8 6 4 2

For every Ivy.

Contents

Ice Floe

Ivy Blake drummed the eraser end of her pencil on page 162 of *Science Grade 5*. A spring breeze reached in the open kitchen window and patted at her face. *Polar bears have no natural enemies, except humans,* she read. She gazed at a photograph of two polar bears standing face-to-face in a snowfield, their arms stretched out to each other. The bigger one rested his paws on the little one's waist; the little one's paws were on the big one's shoulders. He had one leg kicked out to the side like he'd just done step two of the box step, which Grammy had tried to teach her and Prairie last weekend.

Ivy turned the page. *Polar bears depend on ice floes for their survival. They use them to hunt from, live on, and as a place to rest when swimming. The warming of Earth's climate has caused these ice floes to thin and grow smaller.*

In this picture a polar bear stood on an ice floe not much bigger than the front porch, staring at the mountain range that lay in the distance. Ivy put her fingertip on the bear's nose, and then on his porch-sized ice floe. She had a feeling she knew how he felt.

"Ivy!" Prairie called from outside. She was jogging up the path from the barn. "I-*vee*!" She burst into the kitchen, smacking the door up against the inside wall. "What're you doing?"

"Studying."

"*Still?*"

Ivy made an apologetic face.

"But you studied at lunch and on the bus *and* before dinner. How can you stand to study any more? And anyway—" Prairie made a helpless gesture toward the outdoors. Ivy knew what she meant. You didn't need a winter coat, finally.

But studying in the kitchen in the early evening was always one of her favorite parts of the day. The room wrapped itself around you like one of Mom Evers's blankets. Along the walls, there were colorful wooden chairs that Dad Evers had repainted and quilts stacked in piles waiting to be sold at the farmers' market. The windows were filled with plants and Dad Evers's painted birdhouses, and a dusty catnip mouse lay abandoned by her cat, Pup, on the floor. Tonight Mom Evers was working at her sewing machine, Grammy was reading, and every now and then Dad Evers came in for a sheaf of stencils or a smaller paintbrush. It would've been perfect, the hum of the sewing machine the sound track to their quiet industry, except for Prairie. Her cheeks were red, her eyes sparked, she smelled like air and dirt.

"That test tomorrow is not going to be easy, you know," Ivy said. "I just want to do well."

"Well, okay, but can't you take a break? Come outside, I'm making a goat pen."

Ivy smiled at her best friend. Over the winter, Prairie had decided she wanted to raise goats, and she wasn't the kind of person to wait around for the actual animal itself to show up to get started. "In a while, maybe."

Prairie rolled her eyes. "You're going to ace the test, anyway, you always do." She banged back outside and Ivy went back to work. *Polar bears show angry behavior when they lose their prey. They might kick snow or growl when they're disappointed.*

Grammy looked up from her reading. "You have hit those books a good long spell, Knasgowa." *Knasgowa* meant heron, in Cherokee. Grammy was part Cherokee and she had started calling Ivy that over the winter. She called Prairie Tatsuwa sometimes. That meant raven. Other times she called her Saligugi, which meant snapping turtle, and anyone could see why.

Ivy smiled without looking up.

"There is such a thing as overdoing it."

Ivy tipped her head. "But I have to know this stuff. There's a test—"

"Prairie's right, you know. You are going to ace it. You always do."

"Because I *study*."

Grammy rolled her eyes. "That you do. But you also overstudy."

"That's not even poss—"

"A person can overdo anything. It's like exercising too hard. Does more harm than good. I'm not telling you what to do, mind you—"

Ivy made her face very polite but she couldn't help the skeptical glint in her eyes.

Grammy laughed. "I'm just saying, I think you might've hit that magic point where you know the material and ought to just let it simmer away in your brain for a while." She winked and returned to her book, and Ivy went back to hers.

Polar bears look white, but their fur is actually transparent. When light bounces off them, they appear to be the same color as the snow around them. They blend in easily with their Arctic environment.

Ivy drew a little polar bear at the bottom of her notebook page. She sketched an ice floe underneath it, then shaded in the surrounding open water with the side of her pencil lead. She made two mountain ranges out of the words *May* and *June*. May was close; June wasn't very far behind it. June, when the school year ended. On the plus side: the school year ended. And she was going to North Carolina with Grammy and Prairie for a two-week vacation, which was pretty much the most exciting thing she'd ever dreamed of. On the minus side: the school year ended. And then what? What would her mom decide? Would Ivy have to move back in with her and George in Poughkeepsie? Did Ivy even, in a way that made no sense to her, sort of want to?

She studied her drawing, her lips pursed. Then she flopped her books shut and slid them into her backpack. She grabbed her jacket off the hook beside the door and went to find Prairie.

Once she was holding a splintery plank up against a post so Prairie could nail them together, she realized that the best part of her day had just changed, from studying in the kitchen, to this.

Stir Up Some Fun

Saturday night, Ivy sat in the old brick theater in Rosendale with a giant tub of popcorn in her lap. The theater's velvet-covered seats were small and narrow; everybody's arms and elbows banged gently together.

Ivy scooped up a handful of popcorn without taking her eyes from the screen. It was repertory night and the movie, *Hugo*, was about an orphaned boy who lived in the walls of a train station in Paris, France, in the 1930s.

Ivy watched Hugo race through the station, fleeing the stationmaster who'd have him flung into an orphanage if he caught him. Her eyes were wide. If someone had poked her with a pin, she might not have noticed, she was so wrapped up in the story. She felt like she'd ducked under a fence and crossed a border, out of her own life and into his.

• • •

She read the credits at the end of the show carefully. Every hair stylist and prop manager, every gaffer and best boy, every cable puller and coach was a link in the chain it took to make a movie, and the land of making a movie was a place—like a foreign country you yearned to visit— she'd been fascinated by forever. Maybe because her dad had loved movies.

On her right, Grammy leaned forward and squinted. On her left, Prairie tapped her thumb on her knee contemplatively. Beyond her, Mom and Dad Evers sat with their heads tilted at identical angles. Only when the houselights came up did everyone start fishing their arms into their coat sleeves.

"That was a real fine show!" Grammy said as she shuffled past the seats. "I never saw such a contraption as that mechanical man. And those clocks—I guess I never gave much thought to how they work, but now my curiosity's piqued. It'd be fun to get one of those clock kits, see what makes it all tick. Tick—*ha*! Get it?"

Ivy said *uh-huh* as a boy came up the aisle with a broom and dustpan. He was thirteen or fourteen, probably, with tea-colored hair held back in a ponytail. Grammy nodded at him and he smiled as he stopped to let her pass.

You could tell a lot about people even when they didn't say a word, and this boy was nice. It was in his eyes, for one thing, hazel with crinkles at the corners, and in his smile, which started at one side of his mouth and slowly spread across to the other. Also in the way he didn't make a production out of waiting for a slow old lady. Plus, he wore a faded yellow T-shirt that had the Nestlé's Quik bunny on it, saying *Stir up some fun!* Ivy thought that only a really nice boy would wear a shirt like that.

"I didn't know as I'd like a show made for kids, but I did," Grammy boomed. "I liked it fine. I might even come watch it again. Might be up here every night of the week, now you've got me started. Walton and Loren'll have to come pluck me off the seat like a berry off a bush." Her voice got louder every moment, like someone was turning her volume up, and the boy's grin became wide and delighted.

It wasn't like Ivy, really—life had taught her to be cautious— but she smiled back at him. He winked, and in that instant they were friends.

Grammy finally noticed that Ivy wasn't behind her. "Ivy-girl! What're you doing? Get a move on, child, the train's gonna leave the station."

There was no train, really. They'd ridden to Rosendale in the Everses' new-to-them car, and of course Mom and Dad Evers and Prairie wouldn't leave without them.

Ivy took one more look at the boy. He arched his eyebrows. A smile stole out quick from Ivy before she ducked her head and hurried up the aisle.

Blue Plaid Sneakers

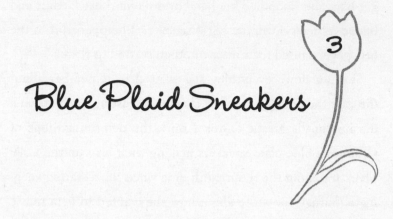

At home, Ivy and Prairie climbed the narrow stairs to their room. Prairie scrambled into the top bunk. "Did you have a good birthday?"

"It was perfect." Pup padded in around the half-open door. Ivy fluttered her fingers at him and he leaped up beside her. She rubbed his ears and he arched his neck and purred. "Thank you for everything. I love the colored pencils."

"You're welcome." Prairie flopped onto her stomach and her arm dangled over the edge of the bunk. "Finally you're eleven too." The arm disappeared. "Now maybe Mom will let us ride our bikes to town by ourselves. Let's ask tomorrow." With each sentence, Prairie's voice grew sleepier, and then she was snoring—snoring lightly, but still snoring, no matter how much she refused to believe it.

Ivy slid the sketchbook Grammy had given her out of its gift bag. She smoothed her hand over its hard black cover and traced a finger down the big wire spiral. She opened it to the first page, paused for a moment, then started to write.

She put down everything she wanted to remember about the day: the orange cake with chocolate frosting, the presents, the boy in the Nestlé's Quik T-shirt, the determined look of Grammy's blue plaid sneakers making their way up the aisle. Then, for about the thousandth time since she'd started keeping a journal, Ivy wrote about how she wanted to be a movie director someday.

It was a crazy dream, but every time she saw a movie, she was filled with the desire. Writing about it used an entire page, and drawing it out with the colored pencils Prairie had given her used another. She drew herself wearing a black beret and carrying a megaphone, sitting in a director's chair with her name on the back of it. It was silly but no one would ever see it, so it was okay.

Ivy wrote and wrote, the notebook on her knees.

She clicked off her light at nine o'clock, the bedtime Mom Evers set for them. At ten she was still awake. Sometimes her thoughts started churning like clothes in a washer and she couldn't stop them. Mom Evers kept saying the baby she was expecting had turned her into the world's lightest sleeper, but Ivy knew she herself was the world's lightest sleeper, really.

Finally she got out of bed and tiptoed into the hall. She peeked into Grammy's tiny bedroom. Empty. She crept to the middle step of the stairs and sat with her arms wrapped around her knees.

"I did enjoy that movie," Grammy said from the kitchen.

"That was something, that train going right through the station wall," Dad Evers said. "Imagine being there *that* day." A fork clinked on a plate. He was having another piece of cake, probably. "You think she had a good birthday?"

"I really hoped her mother would at least call," Mom Evers said. "That woman—"

Ivy tensed, but no one finished the sentence. Pup padded up beside her and she lifted him onto her lap.

Their conversation meandered into the gas mileage the station wagon might get and what time they needed to be at the other farmers' market they went to every week, the one in Woodstock on Wednesday. Ivy listened, thinking about the changes Mom and Dad Evers were making. The new used car, big enough to fit everyone. An addition they were tacking onto the side of the house to be the baby's room. The painted chairs as another thing to sell at the markets along with the flowers and vegetables and quilts and birdhouses, though so far there'd been more money going out on those than coming in. Dad Evers had even taken a part-time job as a mechanic, which bothered Ivy a lot.

She kept thinking if it wasn't for her—an extra person to

feed and clothe—he wouldn't have had to. He'd only taken the job after many late-night talks at the kitchen table, talks they didn't know she was listening to. But it had been her habit ever since she moved in to sit at the top of the stairs if she couldn't sleep and listen to them. Their voices were always low and easy and usually it made Ivy feel like a horse at a trough of cool, clean water, drinking up their conversations.

But now, all the changes made her worry. What would happen to her when the baby came and everything was different?

Thunderstorm

A few nights later, rain drummed on the roof of the farmhouse. Thunder echoed off the mountainside and every now and then a bolt of lightning flashed. Inside, everyone was sleeping. Even Pup was curled behind Ivy's knees instead of stalking the mice that lived in the cellar.

Pup purred, Prairie snored, and Ivy dreamed. She tensed and made a sound of protest. She tried to run and couldn't make her legs move. Something bad was happening, something terrible. She had to stop it—

She woke up thrashing. Her heart pounded, her nightgown was damp with sweat.

"'S just a dream," Prairie mumbled. "'S okay."

Ivy moaned softly "It seemed so real. Like it was happening all over again."

"Take deep breaths."

Ivy did.

"Think of something nice," Prairie murmured.

Ivy's mind felt blank and frightened.

"Want me to come down there?"

"No," Ivy whispered. "I'm okay."

"'Kay. Night, then."

Ivy peered at her clock, the little white travel alarm Aunt Connie had given her so long ago. Both hands were aimed at the twelve. She pulled her quilt closer and gazed into the green-lit darkness.

She was slowly walking through Aunt Connie's living room in her mind, trying to calm herself by looking at everything— brown velveteen sofa, dusty aloe plant, barrel of umbrellas by the door, dragonfly painting over the TV, dragonfly statuettes on the end table, the three metal dragonflies that flew over the archway into the kitchen—when a car that needed a new muffler roared up the dirt road. It squealed into the driveway and brakes screeched. Ivy's eyes flew open. A few seconds later someone was pounding at the kitchen door.

Ivy threw her quilt back and Pup thumped to the floor and stalked away with his tail held straight and stiff. Prairie mumbled something and shoved herself upright. Downstairs there was the low sound of Mom and Dad Evers' voices in counterpoint to the louder, faster sound of Ivy's mother's.

14

By the time Ivy got to the kitchen, Mom Evers was running water in the teakettle, Dad Evers was stirring the embers of the fire, and Ivy's mom was sitting in one of his painted chairs. She wore summer sandals even though it was cold and raining, and her favorite T-shirt (it was clingy and glittery and said *Hot S--t* on it, just like that, with the two dashes in the middle) without a sweatshirt or jacket, plus a pair of jeans Ivy happened to know she hated because she thought they made her look fat, which they didn't. Nothing could; her mom was as skinny as a porch railing. Her hair was damp and her eyes were red and she looked like she'd been awake for about a year straight. "Hey, Ives," she said.

Grammy came in and jerked the belt of her robe tight. "What in tarnation is going on? People are sleeping, for crying out loud, or trying to."

Dad Evers squatted back on his heels. "Tracy's, ah—she's had something of an emergency, Ma."

Grammy yanked her belt even tighter. "There aren't many emergencies can't wait until morning when you come right down to it. I don't see any blood, or limbs missing."

Mom Evers cleared her throat. "I thought I'd make tea. If you wouldn't mind reaching the cups down for me—"

Grammy opened her mouth and clamped it shut again. She marched across the kitchen and yanked mugs from the cupboard. Prairie stepped forward and grabbed Ivy's hand as Ivy's mom swiped her cheeks with her palms. It made her look like a little kid who'd fallen and scraped her knees, and something inside Ivy stopped short. Then her mom erased the sadness from her face—it was like an Etch A Sketch being shaken clean—and started talking.

The gist of it was, she was leaving George. Leaving George, leaving Poughkeepsie, leaving her job at the night desk of the hotel, quitting her life across the river cold turkey. She'd thrown her wedding ring and house keys smack at George's heart, which he didn't have anyway, and pulled away. "I'm all done there. I wouldn't go back if he begged me."

Grammy's spoon clinked in her teacup.

"Gosh," Ivy finally said. "I'm sorry."

Her mom gave a hard bark of laughter. "Don't be sorry for *me*. He's the loser in this deal."

Ivy blinked. "Right. He is. I know that."

"So what do you think?" Her mom trained her eyes on Ivy. Ivy felt like she was standing alone in a tunnel with her. "You want to keep me company?"

"Hang on just a minute—" Grammy began, but Ivy interrupted.

"What do you mean?"

"I figured I'd find a place to rent, get a new job, up in Kingston, maybe. Lindsey mentioned the store at the gas station where she works is hiring."

Lindsey was a friend of Ivy's mom. Ivy didn't like her much, but her mom did, off and on. "You want me to come for a visit, you mean?"

"No, to live."

"You don't wake a child in the middle of the night and talk about moving to another town right near the end of a school year—" Grammy began, but Ivy pulled her hand free from Prairie's and took a step toward her mother and Grammy broke off.

The quiet night sounds of the house—the ticking clock, the humming refrigerator—became quieter yet. The Everses faded into the background until it was only Ivy and her mother, staring at each other.

Ivy thought of that night when she was five. The yelling, the sound of things crashing. Waking up, coming out of her room. Seeing her dad throw something—a bottle? a plate? Ivy never knew exactly what—at her mom.

She had watched her mother's hand pick up a gun from the table. She'd seen her finger pull the trigger, and she'd stared in horror as her dad fell.

It seemed to happen in slow-motion, but of course it really didn't. It happened fast.

Ivy could—just barely—remember that her mom had been different before that night. A little different, anyway. She had a memory of sitting on her mother's lap, curled into her like a snail into its shell. She remembered listening to her mom's heartbeat: *thrum-bum, thrum-bum.* She remembered rocking, and a song being hummed. Every now and then she'd think she heard it on the oldies station Mom and Dad Evers left the car radio set to, but as soon as she noticed, the song would be over.

Ivy thought of the years they'd lived with Aunt Connie in New Paltz, after her father was gone and the judge had ruled what her mom did was self-defense. *Justifiable homicide* was the official term for it. Aunt Connie had sat Ivy down on the couch, her arm around her the whole time, and tried to explain it to her.

Because of Aunt Connie, those years had been good, as good as they could be anyway, after what had happened. But then Aunt Connie got cancer and died too, and Ivy's world had gone pale and dark, until she met Prairie in school.

She thought of how they had become best friends, of Mom and Dad Evers inviting her to live with them when her mom decided to move back to Poughkeepsie with George, as if the past, and Ivy herself, had never happened.

She thought of all this in that time-suspended moment in the kitchen where she'd been so content since last fall, and then she said, "Yeah, Mom. I'd like that."

Saturday morning Ivy's dresser drawers hung open and her suitcase yawned on her bed. She nestled her clock in among her socks so it wouldn't get broken. Prairie stood nearby, scowling.

"I don't want you to move back with your mom. Couldn't you have argued with her?"

The middle drawer held Ivy's jumpers and long johns shirts and leggings. She remembered the day she'd found them at a thrift shop with Prairie, right before school started. Mom Evers had given them each twenty dollars to shop with and then sat outside the changing room while they modeled their choices. She'd nod thoughtfully with her eyes narrowed or else shake her head in pretend horror, making it seem like they were in some fancy department store instead of the resale room at the back of the community center. Afterward they'd gone out for tea and cookies and sat with their shopping bags piled around their ankles, and the whole day had been like something you read about in a book. Ivy's own mom had never done anything like that. She probably never would.

Prairie gave the bureau top a small *whap* with her palm. "Grammy definitely wanted to argue with her. Mom and Dad did too, I know they did."

But Ivy didn't want the Everses having to argue for her, especially not Mom Evers. She had enough to do, with all the work of the farm and the baby coming. Ivy lifted the clothes out of the drawer, taking special care with a dress she'd found that day but had never worn because it seemed too old for her. Mom Evers had said it was okay, though. *It's beautiful,* she'd said, fingering the fluttery, dark blue fabric. *It suits you. Quiet*

19

and elegant. And you've grown so tall these last few months, I'll bet it fits you for a long time.

"You wouldn't have to go if you did. I mean—all the way to Kingston. Starting a new school." Prairie yanked at one of the embroidery-floss ties in Ivy's quilt. Worked it loose and started in on another.

Ivy wanted to pull Prairie's hand away—she loved her quilt, which Mom Evers had made for her, and tried to keep it perfect—but she didn't. "It'll be okay," she said. "It will. It'll be different this time."

White Ice Mint

Ivy scuffed toward the house that her mom had rented on O'Reilly Street, thinking how much she wanted what she'd told Prairie before she moved to be true. In some ways things did seem better. This morning, when her mom asked her to run to the drugstore around the corner and pick up a box of Nicorette to help her quit smoking, she'd made a friendly, gri-macey face, like they both knew it was pretty much hopeless but nevertheless she was going to give it a go—

Things *were* okay. Ivy lifted her chin and walked faster.

The Everses' station wagon glided up to her house as Ivy rounded the corner, and the old pickup loaded with Dad Evers's chairs eased in behind it. Ivy broke into a jog. Prairie jumped out of the car the moment it stopped and she and Ivy flung their arms around each other. Then Mom and Dad

Evers and Grammy were all on the sidewalk and there was a confusion of *Hellos* and *How are yous* and *So this is your house*—

They all turned to look. The house was a small rectangular box covered with graying siding that had popped apart at some of its seams. But with a few nails or some glue, Ivy thought, it could be fixed. With paint—dark green, with cream trim, is what she pictured—and planter boxes spilling out flowers, it would look sweet. Ivy could see it in her head as clear as anything.

But now, with the Everses beside her, she saw something different. The house wasn't sweet. It was just a small, plain carton, the bargain-brand box for storing people in. There were no nails or glue; there would be no paint or planter boxes, at least not while Ivy and her mom lived here. The row of prickly shrubbery that lined the drive—the only outside decoration— had a plastic shopping bag and a paper drink cup caught in it.

Ivy gripped the pharmacy sack harder. "Come on, come in, I have to grab my backpack."

She headed up the walk and the Everses followed. She climbed the shaky wooden steps and went through the front door and everyone came in after her.

"Very nice." Mom Evers rubbed her stomach, smiling.

But it wasn't nice. The inside was as plain as the outside, and maybe a little worse. The white-painted walls were grubby and nicked; the carpeting was a swirl of gray and beige that had probably been designed specifically to hide spills; the couch and chair that came with the place looked stiff and uncomfortable. Also the coffee table was lined with empty beer cans. Last night Lindsey and her boyfriend, Dave, had been visiting and Ivy hadn't had time to clean up before her mom sent her out for the gum.

Ivy glanced at Prairie. Prairie was gazing around unhappily.

"How's your mother?" Mom Evers asked.

"She's, um. She's good, she's fine, she's in the kitchen." Ivy pointed that way and everyone trooped in.

"Hi, Tracy," Mom Evers said.

"Hi."

Ivy handed her mom the bag of Nicorette and her mom stuffed it into her purse. Then she dumped the rest of her coffee down the drain and stubbed out her cigarette in one of Dave's empty beer cans. "Sorry I can't stick around, I have to get to work. I got that job with Lindsey."

"Oh, fine, fine," Mom Evers said in a perky voice. "We can't stay long either, we have to get to the market. Try to sell some things, you know. Hope people are in a buying mood . . ."

Ivy's mother raised her brows. "Good luck." She gave a sketchy wave and headed for the door.

At the market, Ivy and Prairie lugged their folding table to their stall. Ivy breathed in deep as they clumped along. She smelled baked things and food cooking and flowers and plants, fresh air and dampness and wild spring leeks. She started to smile. She already knew what the best part of her day was going to be: this moment, right here, right now.

They set the table up and Ivy snapped their checkered cloth out. Prairie dug in their banana box of supplies for their signs. FRESH FARM EGGS, the biggest one said. SPECIAL! $5.00/DOZEN another announced. They'd had to raise their prices this spring, with the cost of chicken feed going up.

Prairie opened a carton of eggs and put a sign that said EGGS BY PRISCILLA on top of it. Ivy opened another and propped up the EGGS BY SISTER tag. Really, they usually didn't know which hens laid what eggs, but people liked thinking they did.

"Sneaky's getting out again," Prairie said as she set the EGGS BY SNEAKY sign up. "She laid her eggs under the wheelbarrow yesterday. I was lucky to find them. And *muddy*—"

"I'm sorry you have to gather them all yourself." Some of the air hissed out of Ivy's good mood.

Prairie shrugged, busy counting the money they'd open their cash box with. "I don't mind." She tucked the bills into their slots and pushed her hair behind her ears. Then their first customer appeared.

They ate out afterward at the Really Fine Diner. The owner had bought one of Mom Evers's quilts at the market one time, and ever since, she'd bought most of whatever produce they had left at the end of the day, if they brought it around. Their waitress today, Zoe, had curly black hair, blue eyes, and a crooked nose. Ivy always thought Zoe'd be the plucky underdog if she starred in a movie. She grinned at Ivy when it was Ivy's turn to order. "Greek salad? Or is it a cheeseburger kind of a day?"

"Greek salad, please." Ivy smiled shyly.

"Extra banana peppers and olives?"

Ivy nodded.

"Did you get one of those new magnets we have yet?"

"Yes, on the way in. We both did."

"Your home away from home!" Zoe quoted. She tapped Ivy's head with her pen.

Back at the farm, Prairie stuck her magnet on the fridge. She poked Ivy's ribs with one finger. "You've got a couple of homes away from home now. Nice, huh?"

Ivy nodded, even though that wasn't as simple as it sounded. She sat down on the floor and rubbed Pup's belly. He started to purr and Grammy began picking out a soft tune on her banjo. Ivy's shoulders relaxed; she hummed along quietly. Then Dad Evers called for her and Prairie to help him unload, and Ivy scrambled to her feet again. Mom Evers pulled her into a hug as she passed. "It's great to have you here. We *miss* you."

Ivy hugged her gently back, careful of the baby. She let her head rest for a moment against Mom Evers's shoulder and breathed in her familiar smell, of honey and sweat and spices. She smelled like home; the whole house did. It always welcomed Ivy the moment she walked in.

"I-vee!" Prairie yelled from outside. "Help! Can you get the door? I'm dropping stuff all over the place."

Ivy trotted to the door with a choked feeling in her throat. She wondered if the rental in Kingston—and her own mom— would ever feel like home this way.

No lights shone through the front windows when the Everses took Ivy back to Kingston Sunday night.

Mom Evers turned in her seat, worry creased into her forehead.

"My mom's probably asleep already," Ivy said before she could say anything. "She's been working a lot at her new job."

"Sure, but I'll just walk in with you—"

"It's all right," Ivy interrupted in her most cheerful voice. "I've got a lot of work to do. I should've studied more for my spelling test. My new teacher's really tough. I like her though. I like her a lot." This was true; maybe the honesty in her voice was why the worry eased some from Mom Evers's face.

"Okay, then, I guess. Just call if you need anything. I bought you another minutes card." Mom Evers dug the card out of her bag.

Ivy took it and promised she'd call and told Prairie goodbye, but Prairie didn't answer. She was poking the buttons on her cell phone. Ivy had a matching one in her pocket. Mom Evers had bought them when Ivy moved, and while it wasn't fancy—each one had only cost ten dollars—it was precious. It was a small rectangle of connection to the Everses that she kept with her at all times.

"Good luck on your social studies test," Ivy told Prairie.

Prairie kept jabbing at the phone's keypad. "Yeah, thanks. You too."

Ivy frowned. She didn't have a social studies test.

Then Prairie tossed the phone onto the seat beside her and grinned, and Ivy felt her world flip right-side up again. "I'll see you next weekend," Prairie said.

"Bright and early!"

An uncomfortable look flicked across Prairie's face. "Oh, I forgot to tell you—I have a thing on Saturday morning. A 4-H meeting. We're going to Acorn Hill, to see their creamery. So I can't go to the market."

Ivy felt like she'd been punched. She did not belong to the 4-H. Over the winter when Prairie first started talking about goats and goat milk and goat cheese and goat breeds, Ivy hadn't paid much attention. They had chickens, and as far as she could see, they did not need goats. But Prairie disagreed. She disagreed, and then she found a goat club to join.

She'd wanted Ivy to join too but Ivy didn't want to. At the time it hadn't seemed important. She'd been content to stay home and read or draw or just hang out with Mom and Dad

Evers and Grammy. The stove had been hot and the wind had been cold and staying home those nights had been nice. It had seemed right then. It did not seem right at all now.

"Oh," Ivy said when she could. "Okay. Right. Yeah, sure, I get it."

"But you should go. You totally should. I mean, somebody has to sell our eggs, right?"

Ivy's face went pink. "Our" eggs. They weren't really "our" eggs now that Ivy lived in Kingston and did virtually nothing but collect on the profits.

"Mom and Dad will pick you up and I'll be home by the time you get there, or pretty soon after, anyway."

Ivy wanted to say she was busy next weekend too, that she'd forgotten she also had a big important thing to do—

But she couldn't do it. She needed the weekends at the farm. The time was a dose of powerful medicine that would protect her against the rest of the week. "Yeah, okay," she told Prairie. "Saturday afternoon'll be great. I'll see you then." She strode up the walk.

In the kitchen, the same dishes were in the sink as when Ivy left and the same bag of bread sat untouched on the counter. Ivy walked slowly down the hall to her mom's room, letting her fingers trail along the wall the way she did whenever she was in the deep end of a swimming pool.

Her mom was in bed, curled up like a little sea horse. There was a bottle on the nightstand. Half empty, which wasn't so bad. She grumbled in her sleep and curled herself tighter. Ivy tucked the sheet around her shoulders. Then she went and got the box of Nicorette (White Ice Mint, which had sounded like the most refreshing of all the flavors) out of her mom's purse. She tiptoed back in and set it on the nightstand so that it'd be the first thing her mom saw when she woke up.

How to Breathe

6

The most interesting thing about Ivy's second Monday in her new school was that her teacher made them breathe. It was almost time for the bell to ring and a bunch of the boys were throwing spit wads and bouncing up and down in their seats. Ivy was drawing a flower in her notebook. Not just any flower, but the lone tulip that had the guts to come up in their lawn.

You never knew where a flower was going to spring up, she guessed, or what it was going to look like. This one had yellow petals—really yellow, like the color you always made the sun when you were little—and Ivy felt compelled to make a picture of it. Because it was so brave, for one thing. Also because using the pencils Prairie had given her brought Prairie herself right along with them, a little.

She was absorbed in drawing the tulip's leaves when Ms. Mackenzie thwacked her dictionary down on her desk. Everyone jumped. Ms. Mackenzie stood up and loomed over her desk—she was almost six feet tall—and smiled gently. It was funny, once Ivy's heart stopped banging: the *smack* of the dictionary, and then Ms. Mackenzie's tender, pleased smile.

"Dear children. To ensure that you cease this infernal racket, we shall now breathe. For the next seven minutes."

"Breathe?" a girl named Tate asked. She was heavy and had long wavy red hair she always wore loose so it trailed out behind her.

Ivy's own hair was thick and wheat colored, and today she'd done it in one long braid, a braid she pulled over her shoulder and tugged on when she was deep in thought. She tugged on it now. If she ever did make a movie, she'd have a character who looked like Tate. Her hair would stand for her independent nature and fiery spirit. She hadn't really watched Tate long enough to be one hundred percent sure what her nature and spirit were like, but the fact that she was questioning big, bold Ms. Mackenzie made independent seem likely.

"Breathe," Ms. Mackenzie confirmed.

Tate shoved her black-rimmed glasses up with one finger. "Like just—in and out?"

Ms. Mackenzie nodded. "Right. In so your belly inflates like a balloon. Out so it goes flat."

"Oooh, sounds exciting," a boy named Billy Wells said.

Ms. Mackenzie beamed her gaze on him. "It is. It's the most interesting thing ever. And hard too. Most people can't do it."

"Can't breathe."

"That's right. Can't breathe. Not for long, anyway. Not *just* breathe. And certainly not quietly." She made a circle in the air with her pen, like she was circling Billy's face, and gave the center a little poke. Then she pulled the projector screen down and hit a couple of keys on her computer. The stopwatch appeared, set for five minutes. "We've wasted two minutes of all our precious lives. **NO MORE!**" Everybody jumped again.

Ms. Mackenzie smiled the pleased smile. "We have no time to waste. Remember that. When I start this watch, you all start to breathe."

She hit the timer. Everyone started to breathe, out and in, and a great peacefulness swelled up inside Ivy. It was like the time-release film of a seed growing into a tree they'd watched for their science section last week.

7

New Schedule

Her mother's car was gone and the house was empty when Ivy got home from school. The magnet from the Really Fine Diner held up a note. *Lindsey changed my schedule*, it said. *I work three p.m. to eleven now. See you later.*

Ivy's heart went loose in its socket. She stared blankly at the fridge, which was bare of anything but the magnet and the half sheet of notebook paper the note was written on. It never would've been that way when Aunt Connie was alive. Every drawing and gold-starred homework paper Ivy brought home was taped right up and left until there were so many layers you couldn't see the door anymore.

Ivy's footsteps as she walked to her room sounded louder than usual without her mom there. Even though they didn't talk that much, there was always the reassuring presence of someone else breathing and bumping around.

She sat on the edge of her bed with her hands on her knees. Her ears rang, the room was so silent. She wrinkled her nose. The house smelled damp from the crack in the shower wall that had leaked through to the bathroom floor. She'd spent most of her birthday money from Mom and Dad Evers on lemon-scented cleaning liquid and a candle from the drugstore around the corner to try to mask it. She went to her desk to light the candle. It was called Line-Dried Linen and it had almost knocked Ivy over when she held it up to her nose in the drugstore aisle. It smelled just like the laundry after Mom Evers brought it in from outside.

When the candle was flickering, wafting out its homey odor, Ivy felt better. She decided to act like everything was normal and her mom was in the living room watching TV, or in bed napping. First she pulled her books out and did all of her homework. Next she made a box of macaroni and cheese—it didn't taste anywhere near as good as Mom Evers's homemade version, but it smelled almost the same and, like the candle, made the house seem less lonely—and heated the rest of the green beans she'd opened a few days before. Her mom hadn't eaten any of those when Ivy made them to go with their hamburgers Friday night. She'd laughed at Ivy for saying that well-balanced meals were important, but Mom Evers said it all the time and Ivy believed it.

For dessert, she washed an apple and cut it into slices. She ate the wedges slowly, with her eyes closed, pretending she was at the Everses' kitchen table. Then she opened her eyes back up because pretending that made her miss them too much.

Life with her mom was thinner and flatter than life with the Evers, but maybe they just needed more practice. They'd watched TV together Friday night, and laughed in the same places. And when Lindsey called and wanted her mom to go out with her and Dave, her mom had said, *No, I can't, me and Ives are watching a show.*

When the apple was gone, Ivy microwaved a bag of popcorn. She took it to the living room and turned on the Nature channel. A snake appeared on the screen and the narrator's quiet voice explained that the copperhead was native to the southern and southwestern United States but could also be found in southern New England and southeastern New York State, which Ivy knew since twice there'd been a copperhead in the Everses' garden. "The copperhead did not reestablish itself north of the terminal moraine after the Wisconsin glaciation," the narrator said. The foreign-sounding phrases made a calm feeling spread through Ivy.

She slowly munched her popcorn. A love of popcorn was something she and her mom shared and eating it now was comforting. Her mom had brought home not just a single bag or even a whole box of bags but an almost-full case of six-pack boxes from the gas station last week. She'd said that Lindsey said it was almost past its expiration and they might as well divide it up among themselves instead of throwing it out.

Ivy reached her hand into the bag. The copperhead basked in the sun. Then a mouse scuttled by and the copperhead struck and the mouse was dead. Ivy drew her quilt up close with a quick intake of breath, then relaxed again when the snake went back to basking. The world of nature was gory and violent, but also peaceful. There was something reassuring about that.

At nine, Ivy sent herself to bed the same as usual. For the first half hour, she adhered to her lights-out rule and kept the room dark and herself under the covers, but when a yell erupted from the house next door and there was what sounded like someone stumbling across her own porch, she sat up and turned the light on. First that light, and then every light in the house, and then, after a few shaky minutes where she pretended she was brave and strong, she shut herself in the bathroom.

She sat in the tub wrapped in her quilt for the next two hours. At some point during that sweaty, heart-racing time, she remembered Ms. Mackenzie teaching them to breathe: *Balloon belly, flat belly.* She sucked in a wavery but belly-inflating breath, then slowly whooshed it out again.

Her mom got home at eleven thirty and started complaining about Ivy having all the lights on and running up the electric bill, and Ivy went back to bed.

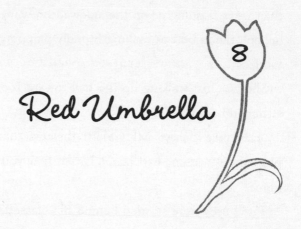

Red Umbrella

8

It started raining that night and poured rain all day Tuesday. At school they had to spend both recesses and lunch hour inside.

It was still raining when Ivy got up Wednesday morning. She peered out the living room window and went back to her closet for her umbrella, an old red one of Aunt Connie's she'd kept when her mom put Aunt Connie's stuff into storage. There'd been a whole barrelful of umbrellas at Aunt Connie's, but this was the one she'd used the most. The rest were extras, *just in case,* she always said when she picked them up at garage sales.

Just in case you're a pack rat, Ivy's mom used to joke.

It was true that Aunt Connie's house had been cluttered, but it had a bustle and cheer to it that was like the Everses', and the big red umbrella always brought that feeling back.

Ivy unfurled it with a flourish when she got out the door, then went sloshing down the sidewalks toward Quail Middle School, the raindrops making friendly plopping noises on the fabric.

She was just walking up the hall toward room 203 as Tate slammed her locker shut.

"Hey, take it easy!" Mr. Caletti, the custodian, roared as he pushed his cleaning cart past. "Is that how you close doors at home?"

Tate's eyes were startled behind her glasses. "Sorry. I guess I wasn't thinking."

Mr. Caletti rubbed his forehead like it ached. "Yeah, yeah. It's no big thing. Just—you don't have to take the thing off its hinges, do you?"

"No, Mr. Caletti. Sorry."

Ivy hung her umbrella on the coat hook in her locker and eased the door shut with extreme caution. It made a very tiny *click*. Tate grinned. After a second, Ivy did too.

"So, what do you think of Ms. Mackenzie?" Tate asked as they walked toward the classroom.

Ms. Mackenzie had a presence as definite as a mountain. She had dark blue eyes and a strong, plain face, and she wasn't pretty, exactly, but she was beautiful. Maybe the most beautiful thing about her was the way she seemed so sure of things. Ivy wished she could be like that. "I like her a lot."

Tate nodded emphatically. "Me too." She flicked a glance

sideways at Ivy. "I noticed you drawing in class. Your flower looked really good."

"Thanks."

"I wish I could draw."

Ivy hugged her books to her chest. "I sort of just do it, I always have. But I could try and show you sometime, if you wanted."

"*Cool*. Holding you to that, Blake." Tate pecked Ivy's shoulder twice with her finger.

At second recess, Billy Wells and Nick Zusak got into a fight in the middle of a kick ball game in the gym. They had their arms clenched around each other's shoulders and Nick, who was much bigger than Billy, almost as tall as Ivy, was pushing Billy toward the table where Ivy was playing a game of solitaire.

"You're a scrawny little *shrimp*," Nick yelled.

Billy's sneakers scrambled. For a second it looked like he was going to get enough steam worked up to change their direction. "You're a—a—a giant *galumph*!" he roared.

The gymnasium, which had gone silent, erupted into laughter.

Ms. Mackenzie sailed onto the gym floor. She dragged the boys apart and marched them away.

"Everyone get out your math books, please," Ms. Mackenzie said after recess.

Everyone flopped their orange *Go Math!* books onto their desks.

"So, we're back to fractions." Ms. Mackenzie drew three circles on the board in red chalk. The class erupted into groans and boos. Ms. Mackenzie spun on her heel. "*Enough*. Pipe down, sit still, and pay attention."

The class went silent.

While everyone was working on their problems, Ivy watched Nick dart his right sneaker forward and whap Billy's shin. Billy whipped around and shoved *Go Math!* off Nick's desk. The book whumped to the floor.

Ms. Mackenzie's head snapped up. "O-kay," she said. "That's it."

Ivy glanced at Tate and Tate looked her way at the exact same moment and they widened their eyes at each other.

Ms. Mackenzie came out in front of her desk and leaned against it. She capped and uncapped the red Sharpie she'd been grading papers with. "We haven't been able to get outside and race around the way we'd like to. Instead of sunshine and softball, we have this." She gestured toward the window, where the rain fell in streaming sheets. "Everyone's a little jumpy, me included. But these things happen. 'Things fall apart; the centre cannot hold.'"

She gazed at the class. Everyone stared back at her dumbly.

Ms. Mackenzie snick-creaked the cap of the marker again. "Frustrations are a fact of life. Maybe you can't figure out what to wear in the morning or maybe it's something much bigger than that."

Ivy froze, wondering if Ms. Mackenzie knew about the terrible things in her life, things that were much bigger than not knowing what to wear in the morning.

But Ms. Mackenzie's gaze swept across everyone, and everyone looked back at her as if they each had a secret they wondered how she'd discovered. "Maybe your friends are changing and you can't figure it out. Maybe *you're* changing and it all seems like too much, too fast. Or not enough, and too slowly." Ms. Mackenzie didn't look at Nick or Billy but they both sat very still. "Maybe your parents are getting divorced or your dog won't behave—anyway, it doesn't matter what it is exactly. You have to figure out how to live through it, okay? Plus, it's spring and it's raining cats and dogs and we all just have to *cope*, right?"

The students gaped at Ms. Mackenzie with their mouths slightly ajar. Ms. Mackenzie frowned like a general in front of a demoralized army. Then she sighed. "Okay. Here's what we're going to do. I want everybody to close their eyes and think about their favorite place. A safe place, a peaceful place. The place you might go—instead of punching someone—if, say, your best friend called you a mean name."

Ivy wondered if Ms. Mackenzie had heard Nick or just made a lucky guess.

"Close. Your. Eyes," Ms. Mackenzie said in a voice like a hypnotist's. "Imagine your place."

Ivy closed her eyes. She could hear Tate breathing in the desk to her left.

"Fill in the details," Ms. Mackenzie murmured.

Ivy saw the red-painted door that led into the Everses' kitchen. She opened it. The big south window was filled with plants. Soup simmered on the stove and rain slashed against the windows. Pup batted his catnip mouse across the floor and it slid under the woodstove. He flattened onto his belly and stuck his paw in to snag it out again. Grammy read in the rocker; Mom Evers worked at her sewing machine; Dad Evers carried in a newly painted chair. Prairie perched at the table making a sign for their eggs, the heel of one boot thumping. Ivy pictured herself next to Prairie.

"Does everyone have someplace imagined?"

Some people nodded, some whispered yes, and Billy Wells yelled, "Does it have to be a real place?"

"Real or imagined, as long as it makes you feel happy. And *calm*." Ms. Mackenzie aimed a pointed look at Billy and Billy nodded. "Okay. Good. Now stay there for a few minutes." She sat down. "Just stay there," she said in the hypnotist's voice.

Ivy peeked and saw that Ms. Mackenzie was grading papers again. She flicked her gaze sideways. Tate's eyes opened and they smiled at each other. Then the bell rang and the room exploded into noise and motion.

"Where'd you go?" Tate asked when they were walking toward their lockers.

"Home. I mean—just to a kitchen I love. Where'd you?"

Tate sighed like someone about to plunge a spoon into a butterscotch sundae. "To the piano in my grandparents' study. Me and my mom live with them since my parents got divorced. My grandfather has a Steinway crammed into his den—he was a concert pianist, a way long time ago—and he lets me play it. It's my favorite thing, next to math. Well, that and singing."

"So—like drawing is to me."

Tate grinned. "Probably."

"I have a guitar, my friend's grandma's been trying to teach me how to play. I'm not good at it so far."

"It takes a while," Tate said.

"I don't think I have the talent."

"Talent's overrated. Practice, practice."

"I don't know—"

"Even just five minutes a day, every day, and you'll get better. Promise." Tate slung her arm around Ivy's shoulder and squeezed it for a second. Then she made a sharp right into the auditorium, where the choir was having an after-school practice.

9
Universal Wire-Bound Sketchbook

At home Ivy's mom sat on the couch flipping through a magazine. It was her day off, but even so Ivy was surprised to see her up. She'd spent most of her free time in bed since they moved here.

Her mom was wearing her *Hot S--t* T-shirt with her favorite jeans. Her right leg was jiggling like it was going somewhere even if the rest of her stayed put. She looked up when Ivy came in. "Hey," she said.

"Hey."

"How was school?"

Ivy's eyes widened. "Okay."

Her mom smacked the magazine shut. "Want to go for a drive?"

"Sure, if you want to."

"I wouldn't have said so if I didn't."

Ivy picked her bag up again—her notebook and pencils were in it and she didn't like to go anywhere without them—and followed her mother to the car.

They roared out of their neighborhood in the Mustang. Her mother drove swiftly toward the north side of town and Ivy wondered where they were going. To one of the parks on the river, maybe. She hoped so. But then her mother crossed the bridge and got on the highway south to Poughkeepsie and Ivy's heart tightened.

"Cute town," her mom said flatly as they drove through a little village with narrow streets.

"Yeah." A fancy coffee shop, an antique store, and a gelato place slid by.

They stopped at a light, and her mom turned the radio up so loud the car almost shook. She gave the gas pedal a quick hard shove and made the engine roar, and the people waiting at the crosswalk turned to look. She roared away when the light turned green. "Give 'em a dose of the real world. Which this is not, believe me."

"Mmm," Ivy said. It *was* the real world. Ivy could've reached out and touched every bit of it: the gold-plate letters of ANTIQUE SHOPPE, the curved backs of the wrought-iron chairs in the gelato place, the silky fabric of the dress a woman on the corner wore, the springy fur of her tiny dog.

Ivy was glad when they left the town behind, but nervous

again when they reached the north side of Poughkeepsie. Her heart shriveled as they approached George's neighborhood.

"Mom?"

Her mom downshifted.

"What are you doing?"

Her mom eased the car into the turn for George's street. "Lindsey called from work. She said George came in with some brunette. Like he was trying to flaunt her in my face, only I wasn't there."

"Mom—"

"It's only been a few weeks, it really steams me."

Ivy clutched the door handle. She wished she had the courage to suggest to her mom that she find a safe place to go inside her head instead of coming here.

"Whoops!" her mom said when she clipped George's mailbox two minutes later. The mailbox tilted backward but didn't fall all the way over. "Guess I got a little too close." She hit the gas and sped away. Ivy glanced around, but as far as she could tell, there was no one to have seen. She sank down in her seat anyway.

She only inched up when they'd crossed the Hudson again and her mom pulled into a restaurant parking lot. She flicked off the ignition and the key ring clacked. It was a string of translucent beads in different colors that spelled out T-R-A-C-Y. "I don't feel like cooking."

Ivy unclipped her seat belt. She wondered if it was coincidence that they'd pulled into the Really Fine Diner. She loved the Really Fine, of course. She'd come here with the Everses so much that she knew most of the waitresses by name—Zoe, Olympia, Margot, and Susan. But she'd never been here with her mother. Ivy glanced at her. She was riffling through her purse for a piece of Nicorette. She fished one up and began chewing it like a starved person. "Ready?"

Ivy nodded. Her stomach was churning.

Zoe led them across the room and they passed Ms. Mackenzie at a table crowded with people. Ms. Mackenzie leaned toward a man with large ears and pointed at him with her fork. She was having the Greek salad, Ivy noticed with a spark of pleasure. Ms. Mackenzie grinned when she saw Ivy. "Hey! I know you!"

"Hello," Ivy said shyly. Suddenly, she felt happier. Ms. Mackenzie tapped her plate with the fork she'd been pointing at the big-eared man. "The best Greek salad in town."

"I *know*. It's my favorite too."

At the table, Ivy studied her menu even though she always got either a cheeseburger or a Greek salad, and then Zoe came and took their order. Five minutes later, her mom's face had turned dark. She drummed her fingers on the tabletop. "This is taking too long."

"I'll bet it comes soon, though. It's usually pretty fast here."

"Is that so? Your precious Everses bring you here, is that it? Take you out to eat all the time like it's nothing?"

Ivy took a sip of tea instead of pointing out that the Everses sold their produce here.

The food came a minute later. Ivy poked an olive onto her fork and ate it in two bites, then mashed a chunk of feta onto a few spinach leaves and munched that down. She looped a circle of onion and a banana pepper onto her fork next and speared another olive. She wished her mom would start eating too.

Finally her mom took a bite of chicken strip. She put it down. Ivy looked at her through lowered lashes and kept eating. Grammy would've told her she was eating too fast, if she'd been there.

When Zoe came by and asked how everything was, Ivy said good at the same time as her mom said *terrible*. "The fries are burnt, they're inedible, and the chicken strips are no good, they don't taste right, they're spoiled or something. Plus they're cold. It's ridiculous."

Zoe's face went slack with surprise. "I'm sorry, ma'am, but I don't think that's possible. Those fries are not burnt, and as far as the chicken, I've been serving it all afternoon and no one else has complained. And they can't be cold, either, I watched the cook pull them out of the fryer."

"Bull," Ivy's mother said fiercely.

Ivy dropped her fork. It clattered onto her plate and an

olive rolled onto the table. Her mom whipped her head around and stared at her like she'd done an unimaginably bad thing. Fortunately—or not so fortunately, depending on how you looked at it—she was too mad at Zoe to concentrate on Ivy for long. She said a lot of things; her words were like a swarm of hornets. The bottom line was, she wanted to leave without paying for her meal or Ivy's, even though Ivy's Greek salad—which Zoe had been nice enough to add extra banana peppers and olives to without Ivy even asking—was perfect.

"I can't do that," Zoe said. "But how about I give you your meal and a dessert, and everyone can part ways with no hard feelings?"

"Not good enough."

Ivy shot Zoe an agonized look and Zoe gave her a quick grim smile before she turned her attention back to Ivy's mom. "I'm sorry you feel this way, ma'am, but I'm not comping both meals. I'll get my manager—"

Ivy's mother picked up Ivy's notebook, the artist's book Grammy'd given her for her birthday that said *Universal Wire-Bound Sketchbook* on the front cover sticker, and hurled it at the wall.

The pages flared open. Zoe hopped sideways. Ivy didn't wait to see what would happen next. She bolted for the exit. She stumbled on something as she rushed past Ms. Mackenzie's table, but yanked her foot free and kept moving.

She tried not to look at anyone. Maybe that little-kid fantasy that anyone you didn't see couldn't see you would work. But to her horror, just before she got through the dining room, she saw the boy from the theater in Rosendale. He was at a table with an older couple, his parents or grandparents probably. He looked right at her and Ivy could tell he recognized her.

Her cheeks flamed. She hurtled out the door.

10

Zigzag

Ivy hurried across the parking lot. She didn't know if her mom was right behind her or still inside yelling at Zoe, or if the police would come or what. She glanced over her shoulder. Ms. Mackenzie stood under the diner's awning, her hand shielding her eyes. The boy from the theater was coming out the door behind her.

Ivy ducked behind a tan pickup truck and peered through the tinted windows of its topper. Ms. Mackenzie wore a red scarf printed with white polka dots, a white T-shirt, and a pleated red skirt. She'd probably been celebrating some special event with all those people. A birthday or an anniversary. Ivy grimaced. It was even worse to interrupt something like that than just a regular dinner. Ms. Mackenzie walked out into the lot and Ivy went statue-still. After a moment, Ms. Mackenzie shook her head and turned back toward the diner. At the door, she said something to the boy from the theater, then went inside. The boy took one more look around the lot and then he went in too.

Ivy sagged against the truck. She felt both disappointed and relieved. And most of all, tired. Too tired to hide behind a stranger's truck anymore.

She walked slowly to the Mustang. It wasn't locked. Her mom always said they didn't have anything worth stealing and, if someone did take something, they must need it pretty bad. She probably only said that because the locks didn't work, but maybe she really did mean the part about someone else needing their stuff. Her mom surprised her sometimes. Not usually in a good way, but sometimes. Ivy got in and sat with her head down, holding her hands together to keep them from shaking.

What she wanted to do: walk out of the parking lot and keep walking forever, walk until she was eighteen years old and could start her own life.

She took a sharp breath and huffed it out, then another.

After a while her mother appeared, and they roared from the lot. Apparently the police were not coming.

If she'd had her notebook on the way home, Ivy would've drawn a towering stack of boxes all tumbling down. She stared out the window and considered what the best part of her day had been, instead. She finally decided it had been Zoe saying,

"You want your usual?" and bringing a silver pot of hot water and the wicker basket of tea. Zoe'd grinned when she noticed the Lemon Lift tag dangling over the edge of Ivy's cup. "My favorite too," she'd said.

"I'm sorry about your notebook thingy," Ivy's mom said as she turned onto O'Reilly Street. "I'll get you another one."

Ivy had no idea how to respond.

Nothing could fix the wrongness of what her mom had done. Nothing could change her sudden fury at Zoe, her hand grabbing Ivy's sketchbook—which was *hers,* a part of her, a gift and a quarter full of writing and drawing and the start of a story she was trying to write about an orphan girl named Heather Lake—and flinging it at the wall.

But at the same time, her mom had never said *I'm sorry* to Ivy before. The words were like some strange creature from the bottom of the deepest part of the ocean.

Black Hole

Ivy didn't go to school the next morning. She didn't even ask her mom if she could stay home, she just did it. Her mom stayed in bed until almost noon, and when she got up, Ivy said, "I didn't feel good," and picked up her peanut butter and jelly sandwich and carried it to her room.

She didn't go to school Friday, either. She watched television until her mom got up. Then she went into her room until her mom left for work. Her mom hardly spoke to her. Since that apology and Ivy's nonresponse, her silence had become full of injury, like Ivy was the one who'd done something mean instead of the other way around.

For the first time ever, Ivy didn't try to smooth things out between them.

• • •

Friday afternoon Ivy realized there was no way she could go to Prairie's house for the weekend. At three fifteen she went out on the front step with her cell phone.

"I'm sick," she said. "I can't come this weekend."

There was a surprised silence. Then Prairie said, "Oh. Okay. Well, but—I could bring you ginger ale or something instead of going to the creamery. I could even bring one of those coloring books you like—"

"They're not *coloring* books."

"Well, design books, whatever, the ones they have at the art store—"

Ivy grimaced, sorry for snapping. "They're expensive though."

"Yeah, but I want to. So you'll have something to do. Being sick is so boring."

"I know, thank you, but, you'd better not." Ivy tried to sound grateful but really she only wanted the conversation to be over. "I think I'm contagious. I've been throwing up. I don't even feel good enough to read or draw or anything. All I want to do is sleep."

There was another deep silence. It was as if Prairie knew she was lying, though Ivy didn't know how she could've. Finally Prairie said, "Um, sure. Okay. I'll see you next weekend, then. Get better. Feel better."

"I will. Thanks." Ivy made her voice sound weary, which wasn't hard.

She went inside and turned the television on. She kicked

the couch on her way past, even though it hadn't done any-thing but give her a place to sit. She hurt her toe doing it.

Her mom drank a cup of coffee while Ivy stared at the toaster waiting for a piece of bread to toast Saturday morning. Her mom was subbing for Lindsey and working a double shift, so she was up before usual. The toast popped up and Ivy took it to the couch.

Ten minutes later her mom was by the door shoving her feet into her clogs. She slung her purse over her shoulder. "Don't leave every light in the house on when you go to bed tonight. Heat up a can of that soup that's in the cupboard or something."

"Okay." Ivy gazed at the TV. Her mother banged out the door.

Ivy glared at the television and then turned it off. In her heart, she hoped the car would stop, turn, and screech back down the street, that her mom would barge in and yell, "Hey, get yourself up off that couch and do some homework or something, and what's this about you staying here this week-end? You never stay here on the weekend for one thing, and I have to work for another. This is no good, we can't have it. Get your rear in gear."

Of course that didn't occur.

Ivy was now a truant and her mother was going to pretend that nothing was happening. It was what she always did. The bad things that went on—bad things *she did*—were supposed to vanish, evaporate like water on hot concrete. Instead, Ivy thought, they went into a black hole. It was a place that might not be visible or audible, but it was real, and powerful. It would suck you in and devour you.

12

A Girl

That afternoon Ivy padded into her mother's bedroom.
The blankets were pulled tight and the throw Aunt Connie had
given her mom for Christmas one year—fleece with a print of
pussycats all over it—was folded in half across the foot. That
her mother always made her bed no matter what was one of
the surprising things about her. Ivy sat on the edge of the mat-
tress and dangled her feet, not very far. She was almost as tall
as her mom now.

When a car pulled into the drive, Ivy jumped. Then there
was a tapping on the door. Ivy got under Aunt Connie's cat
blanket and pretended she was a girl who was too sick even to
move.

She actually pretended this—as if she was a character in a
movie, "a girl," instead of herself, Ivy. It helped for about as

long as the knocking lasted. When the car pulled away, she felt like she'd been flung to the farthest corner of the universe and would never find her way home. She let tears seep out of her eyes, and slowly, she reached out and lifted the bottle that was beside her mom's bed.

She twisted the lid off and smelled. Put a finger down in the bottle and tilted it until liquid sloshed onto her finger. She watched three minutes lurch by on her mother's bedside clock while she thought about trying it.

Then she put the bottle back exactly where it had been and rushed to the kitchen and washed her hands. Next she stuck her head under the tap and let the water run over her tongue even though she hadn't tasted from the bottle.

Sometime while the water gushed into her mouth and ran into her hair and splashed across her face, Ivy decided she was going to school Monday morning. She was going to have to face it all and get on with her life.

She called Prairie late on Sunday night. "I feel a lot better. It was *so* boring. All I did was sleep and watch TV. Ugh."

"We stopped by—"

"Did you?" Ivy said brightly. "Wow, I didn't know. I slept a lot."

"I knocked for a long time."

"Huh."

"You must've been pretty sick, not to hear it."

"I was. It was no fun."

"We ate at the Really Fine."

Ivy froze like a mouse about to be snapped up by a copperhead.

"I had a cheeseburger. Of course."

There was laughter in Prairie's voice and Ivy laughed too. She hoped Prairie wouldn't notice how shrilly it came out. "Of course!"

"Olympia waited on us. She asked where you were."

"Uh-huh?" The mouse-at-the-end-of-its-life feeling swept over Ivy again.

"We told her you were sick and she tried to send a cup of tea home with us. She thought you were my sister."

"Oh!"

"Which you are, of course, blood sisters, like we swore," Prairie said. "It's just—she thought you lived with us."

"Uh-huh."

"I wish you did. I miss you."

Tears rose in Ivy's eyes. "Me too."

"Why don't you come home, then?"

Ivy's feelings did a tailspin. It was like when her mom apologized for throwing her notebook. One moment Ivy'd felt one way and known it was the right and only way. Then, a few words later, everything was changed. The situation was completely different, and yet there was something identical about it. "I *am* home."

"You know what I mean." Prairie's sigh was vexed. "I just

mean that we all miss you. We want you here, when the baby comes and everything. You're ours, that's how we feel. Me and Grammy and Mom were talking about it last night and we all agreed. Even though you're not ours, of course, we know that. You're your own person. But you're *our* own person, if that makes any sense."

"Thanks," Ivy said thickly. She should add something more, but she couldn't. She didn't know what it would be. She thought of lying in bed with Aunt Connie's blanket pulled up, pretending to be "a girl." *What girl* was the question she couldn't seem to answer.

"Well—I'm glad you're feeling better," Prairie said after a few seconds had ticked by. "That's good."

"It was a rotten weekend."

"Should've let me bring you that ginger ale."

"You're probably right," Ivy said.

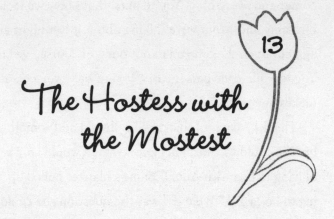

The Hostess with the Mostest

Monday morning, Ivy scuffed down the front steps, her backpack heavy on her shoulders. The tulip in their yard had blown apart in all the rain, and the words Ms. Mackenzie said last week slid into Ivy's brain: *Things fall apart; the centre cannot hold.* It sounded like poetry. She'd have to look it up next time she was in the library. She sighed and plodded onward.

All through the first half of the day Ivy kept her head down and her mouth shut and tried to think herself invisible. At lunchtime she headed for a table at the far side of the cafeteria. She sat with her back to the room and took her sandwich out of her sack. The peanut butter tasted like salty glue. The cherry jam her mom had brought home from the gas station tasted like corn syrup. Her lie that she'd been sick over the weekend seemed to be coming true. She didn't feel good at all. When the sandwich was half gone she took out her banana. It was soft. She pulled the peel halfway off, then sat looking at it glumly.

"Oh, yum." Tate slid onto the bench across from her. "I love old bananas. I never get one. My grandma always turns them into banana bread, which I hate. Isn't that dumb?"

"Um—no. You like what you like, everybody does."

Tate took an apple out of her bag and polished it on her shirtsleeve. She was about to take a chomp out of it when she suddenly stuck it out toward Ivy. "Want to trade?"

Ivy's eyes widened. "Really?"

"If an apple a day keeps the doctor away, I should be set for life. It's all my mom ever puts in."

Ivy held out the banana and took Tate's apple.

"Hurrah!" Tate took a bite, and said, still chewing, "Don't tell my grandma, she'll be mushing it up with walnuts and flour quicker than you can say spit."

Ivy started. "My friend Prairie says that."

"'Quicker than you can say spit?' She must be good people, then."

Ivy nodded and chomped into the apple, which was crispy and tart and perfect.

By the end of the day she thought life was going to go on more or less as usual despite what had happened at the diner. But as she was walking past Ms. Mackenzie's desk, Ms. Mackenzie said, "Ivy, I'd like to talk to you."

Ivy stared at the three small pottery jugs that sat on a corner of the desk. Ms. Mackenzie had pencils in the orange one, pens in the blue, and dry-erase markers in the green. The jugs were curvy and squat and their colors were bright but not too glaringly bright. They were nice.

"It won't take long."

Ivy wondered how you'd draw the pots to show how the light caught their curved edges.

"Ivy?"

The room smelled of the glue they'd been using to paste up their geography projects before the bell rang. Ivy's was a collage about the Himalayan mountains. Cutting the pictures out of magazines, looking for the right shapes and colors, she had felt like she'd left one room of herself and entered another, a bright airy room. She was back in the first room now, though. The dark, stuffy one. Out in the hall, someone in heels clicked by.

"Very seventies, don't you think?"

Ivy looked up. "What?"

"The jugs. They're from a chip-dip set my parents got when I was a kid. They sat in the center of a wire basket. You put your chips in the basket and your dips in the tubs, and voilà, you were the hostess with the mostest."

"Oh." Ivy tugged on her braid.

Ms. Mackenzie swung the chair beside her desk around so it was facing her own, and motioned Ivy into it. "Sit," she said.

Ivy sat.

"If you need me to call your mom and explain why you're staying after, I will. If you need a ride home, I'll arrange it."

Ivy stared at her shoes. She was wearing the black granny boots she'd found the same day she found all the dresses and long johns shirts with Mom Evers and Prairie. The boots were too big, but she'd told herself that just meant she'd grow into them and get to wear them longer.

"Ivy?"

Her mom wouldn't like being called from school. Also Ivy didn't need a ride. She bumped one toe against the other.

"Do you need me to call anyone or arrange a ride home?"

Ivy shook her head. "I walk to school."

"All right, then." Ms. Mackenzie furrowed her forehead and studied Ivy like Ivy was a painting, or a math problem. Ivy squirmed, then made herself sit still. Soon Ms. Mackenzie would start asking sympathetic questions that Ivy did not want to answer, like *how often was her mom's temper so bad,* and *did she always throw things when she got angry* (no, not always; sometimes she did even worse things), and *did Ivy want to talk about it.*

The answer to that would also be no.

But Ms. Mackenzie didn't say any of that. Instead she opened her desk drawer and pulled Ivy's sketchbook out and handed it to her.

Ivy gasped, then grabbed the book and held it tight against herself.

"I picked it up right away. No one else even touched it."

A great heaviness lifted out of Ivy.

"I have to admit something to you, however."

Ivy gazed at her, waiting.

"No one else looked at it, but I did."

The sick feeling roared back. Ms. Mackenzie had seen her attempts to draw a twist of ribbon until one actually *looked* like a ribbon, which had taken pages and pages. She'd seen the drawing of Ivy's and Prairie's legs and feet and grocery bags, which Ivy had done while riding in the way back of the station wagon. You might not expect that four grocery bags and two sets of legs and two pairs of holey tennis shoes could be interesting, but they were. The drawing always brought the day back: the smell of peaches, the leafy green of the big bunch of parsley hanging out of the bag, the peaceful feeling Ivy had inside, the song Prairie hummed to herself—*Oh, my darling, oh, my darling, oh, my daaar-ling Clementine.* Now she didn't know why she'd been so pleased with it—a lopsided drawing of groceries!

Worst of all were the pictures she'd drawn of Ms. Mackenzie, and the one of herself as a movie director. That dumb, dumb beret; that ridiculous megaphone; that awful chair with her name on it.

Ms. Mackenzie folded her hands and looked solemn. "I apologize for doing that. I shouldn't have, but I couldn't stop myself."

Despite Ivy's resolve, a tear, a stupid, stupid tear, brimmed.

Ms. Mackenzie touched Ivy's shoulder. "Ivy, your drawings are great. They really are."

Ivy flicked a quick questioning glance at her.

"I didn't read anything after the first few words—I could see it was private—but I looked at the pictures. They're *so* good. Ivy—wow!"

Ivy closed her eyes; a shiver ran over her.

"Look at me."

Despite herself, Ivy opened one eye and then the other. Ms. Mackenzie was gazing at her, her expression intent. "Listen. You're interesting, and you're smart and strong. You're going to go far. You are. You just must never give up."

Goose bumps raised on Ivy's arms. She flicked her eyes back to the toes of her boots. Round black toes with scuff marks. They were friendly in the same way as the little pots.

"Ivy. I want you to know this. You can do something with your life, no matter what may've come before."

So all her hoping that here no one would know her history had been foolish. Of course they knew. It was in her records.

"*Ivy.*"

Ivy jumped.

"*Listen.* You can make something of your life, and you will. You already have."

"Right," Ivy said.

"It's true. You can do whatever you want to. Don't let anything defeat you. Do you hear me?"

Ivy sat as still as a wild animal in the woods.

Ms. Mackenzie gave a great booming laugh then, a laugh like you'd expect out of Santa Claus on his best day ever, Santa on vacation in Florida, basking in the sun on some secluded beach where he could let his hair down instead of driving all over in a cold sleigh delivering heavy packages. "I know you do hear me. And there's something I want you to do for me this summer."

Ivy shook her head, like she had water in her ear. "Summer?"

"You know—summer. Sun, sleeping in, no school, that whole scenario?"

After a pause, Ivy nodded. Summer with the Everses would probably have been like that. Not exactly—there was a lot of work on the farm in the summer, a lot of markets to pack up for and unpack from—but similar. It would have felt safe and carefree in a way in which life with her mom mostly didn't.

Actually, always didn't, even when things were going all right. Once you began to distrust something, the wariness was always there, waiting to leap out.

"There's only a couple weeks of school left, vacation's almost upon us. I want you to amaze yourself. Follow your dreams. That's the answer."

"I didn't ask a question," Ivy dared to say, though she was looking at her hands and said it quietly and politely.

"Yes, you did. You most certainly did."

Ivy's eyes inched up. Ms. Mackenzie wiggled her brows. "Promise me."

Slowly, Ivy nodded.

She stopped when she was almost out the classroom door. "How?"

Ms. Mackenzie tilted her head.

"How do I amaze myself? What do I do, how do I start?"

Ms. Mackenzie tapped her pen on her blotter. "Start anywhere, you already have." She pointed at the sketchbook. "There's the evidence. You're great at seeing things. That's a gift."

Ivy squinted at Ms. Mackenzie. "Just—seeing? That's a thing? A special thing, I mean?"

"Trust me. It's like breathing. Everybody thinks it's so easy, but it really isn't. It's a talent. And you have it."

"So—"

"Draw more pictures, make a movie, whatever you want. Just, whatever you do, *don't quit*."

Ivy nodded.

"I liked that picture of you as a director. Pretend your eyes are a camera. Turn them on and let them roll: lights, camera, action."

14

Lights, Camera, Action

Ivy scuffed toward home along the cracked sidewalks. It was weird to think that noticing was a talent. It just seemed natural, like breathing. How could you not notice the way the gold of the afternoon sun made the old houses along the street look stately and dignified instead of old and shabby the way they did on cloudy days? How could you not notice the smell of oil on pavement, or the way the damaged letters in the coffee shop's sign made it seem to say FAKED GOODS instead of BAKED GOODS?

An elderly couple came out of the coffee shop together. The woman wore pink pedal pushers and the man had on a blue plaid shirt and brown leather shoes. His hands shook as he took his wife's arm; she wrapped a hand over his and they moved slowly down the sidewalk together, their bodies turned slightly toward each other. If Ivy was making a movie to define one word, she'd film them and call it *Love*.

She shoved her hands into her dress pockets and smiled to herself. Her boots made a *click-scrff* sound as they hit the pavement.

A few blocks from home, she stopped to admire a house she liked. It was old, two stories, painted white, with a long glassed-in porch and a turret going up on one corner. Every time she stopped she imagined how it would be to live there. It seemed like it would be wonderful. Romantic, somehow. And peaceful. The yard had a wrought-iron fence around it and tulips and daffodils blooming everywhere. Wind chimes tinkled, a gazing ball gleamed on an iron stand, a bird flittered at the edge of a birdbath. Some days she'd see a lady in the garden, or on the porch. Today the porch door was ajar—it often was—and Ivy saw a swing, some wicker furniture, a huge blue-and-white vase full of flowers, and—this was new—one of Dad Evers's chairs.

She yanked her phone out of her pocket and jabbed Speed Dial for the Everses—theirs and Prairie's were the only numbers programmed in—and waited for someone to pick up. No one did, but that wasn't surprising. Prairie would be on her way home from school, Mom and Dad Evers were probably busy outside, and Grammy could be anywhere—helping them, or volunteering at the library in town, or playing her banjo so loud she didn't hear the phone ring.

Ivy left a message: "Hey, it's me! I'm walking home from school, and I see one of Dad's chairs on someone's porch. It looks great there! Really great. Also, I wanted to tell you I'm feeling better. I can't wait to see you all on Saturday!"

She clicked the phone off, grinning. Here was a case of noticing and doing something about it: *lights, camera, action,* like Ms. Mackenzie said.

Claim to Fame

15

Two police cars were parked in the driveway behind her mother's Mustang when Ivy rounded the corner of O'Reilly Street a few minutes later. She stopped short. She wanted to go straight back to Quail Middle School. She even turned halfway around to do it. Maybe Ms. Mackenzie would still be there, and Ivy could—

Ivy could what? Go home with her and pretend her real life wasn't happening? That wouldn't do any good.

She took a deep breath and began walking forward. One thing she'd decided a while ago—well, when Aunt Connie got sick and died so fast, before they had time to believe it was really going to happen—was that, no matter what, she would be brave and face things. It was going to be her claim to fame, even if no one but her ever knew about it. It was a private promise she'd made to herself and to Aunt Connie.

She walked past the blue house with white trim. Past the brick duplex. Past old Mrs. Phillips from next door, who knelt on a folded-up sweater pulling weeds from her flower beds. The beds were so close to the sidewalk that Ivy could've reached out and touched Mrs. Phillips's shoulder. Mrs. Phillips gave her a sympathetic look. Ivy met her gaze and pulled her mouth into a worried smile, then lifted her chin and kept going.

Two policemen stood in front of the front door with Ivy's mother, and two sat in the second car. The two in the car turned their heads toward Ivy when she walked up. The window rolled down. "Where are you going, young lady?" the man in the driver's seat asked. His face was chiseled and square; his hair was buzzed short. If you grabbed a stock policeman out of a lineup at a movie audition, he'd be it.

Ivy nodded at the house. "I live here." She took a step forward.

"We'll go with you." The window rolled up again.

Ivy stood with her shoulders slumped. This was her own house. A rental, maybe, and nothing special, but her own. The place she came back to with her pencils and sketchbook, the place she slept and dressed and ate in, the place where she kept the stones she picked up on Skytop, the overlook on the mountain near the Everses' farmhouse, whenever she and

Prairie hiked there. She didn't want to wait for someone else to tell her she could walk up to it. She did wait, however. It seemed like she had to.

Both men climbed out of the car and shifted their feet to straighten the creases of their pants legs. The three of them walked toward the door and Ivy's mom's eyes locked onto Ivy.

"My daughter's home, you have to go," she told the officers. "I don't want her getting upset." She reached an arm out.

Ivy went to her and her mom pulled her close. Ivy let herself sink back and remembered being curled into her mother's chest when she was small. Her mom's chest was bony now; it was like leaning onto rocky ground. Familiar ground, though.

"This is just a matter of following up on a complaint," the nearest man said. "Mr. Gillman says that last week his garbage cans were spread all over the street. Then somebody ran his mailbox over. And now his car's got a brand-new dent in the fender. He's thinking it's you. And he says you've been calling late at night and hanging up when he answers."

Her mom's grip tightened. "Well, boo hoo for him, and tell him to prove it. There's a lot of people got a lot worse problems than a broken mailbox and a ringing telephone."

"So you did run his mailbox down, is that what you're saying? You have been calling?"

"I'm not saying anything. I had my fill of George Gillman a while ago. I left in April and I haven't seen him since."

"But you have seen his mailbox? And his car?"

Her mom's arms went tighter around Ivy than ever. Her breath was a desert wind in Ivy's ear.

The nearest policeman smiled sympathetically, though maybe that was an act. "Listen, I know how it is. A relationship goes south, things are said, your feelings get worked up, maybe you want to leave him a message, something to remember you by. But it's not worth it. Especially not to a woman like you. You've got a history—"

"Hey, that was ruled justifiable, you can't go bringing it up. I'll get a lawyer and sue for harassment if you—"

"You need to leave your ex alone," the man broke in. "Don't make us come out here again. Like you said, you have your daughter to think of."

All the officers' gazes shifted to Ivy. Their eyes were all different: brown, blue, wide-set, narrow, but Ivy saw that to each of them, she was a zero. At worst, she was just like her mom. At best, she was innocent but doomed.

"I didn't make you come out here. George Gillman did that, and he better knock it off. I'm living in a whole different town, minding my own business, and he sets the cops on me. I won't stand for it—"

Her mom said more, but Ivy tuned it out. She turned herself into a block of wood that hadn't been carved yet. She hadn't been carved, there was still time, she could become something beautiful and good.

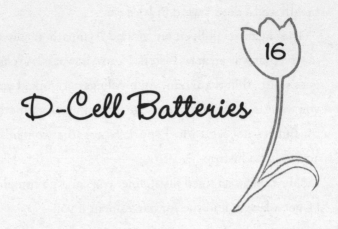

16

D-Cell Batteries

Ivy hauled four outfits out of her closet in the morning and spread them across her bed. She considered each in turn: a denim jumper, a plaid skirt with pleats, a polka-dotted dirndl, and the elegant dress of fluttery dark blue material that she'd fallen in love with at the thrift shop last fall.

Finally she pulled that one over her head. She was going to follow Ms. Mackenzie's advice. She was going to amaze herself. She was not going to be beaten and she was not going to *look* beaten. She was going to look as good as possible. And as old as possible. She'd be *in character*—in the character of an eighteen-year-old, say, who was in charge of her own life.

When the dress's last glittery rhinestone button was done up, Ivy pulled on a pair of black tights and laced up her granny boots and clumped down the hall.

She studied herself in the bathroom mirror. She thought she looked older than usual, but if she used her mom's eye makeup, she would look older yet.

She did this, then added a swipe of lipstick and made kissy lips at herself. Next she put on a hat she'd found abandoned at a farmers' market. It was made of navy-blue straw with a narrow brim and had a white satin ribbon around the band. She adjusted it, then nodded at herself and ran to the living room for her book bag.

Ms. Mackenzie stared when Ivy came through the door. "Wow," she said. Ivy's heart fell. Then she said, "You look lovely, Ivy, but you do have to take your hat off in class," so Ivy did.

Tate came in and thunked *Go Math!* on her desk. She looked Ivy up and down and whistled. "Holy cats. You look like a million bucks."

Ivy's face flushed; she tugged on her braid. Then she remembered what she'd decided in her room. She lifted her nose and pooched her lips at Tate. She fluttered her eyelashes too, but they got stuck in the mascara, which maybe she'd put on too thick.

Tate laughed. "So what's the outfit for, anyway?"

"Nothing, really. Just to do it. Just to be—different."

"Different." Tate tapped her bottom teeth with her thumbnail. "I like it."

Ivy felt a rush of affection for her. "Also, I thought, maybe—it'd be like making a character. Did you ever think about that? How you don't always have to just be you? You can, sort of, make somebody up and be them."

Tate squinted at her worriedly.

"Like in a movie, I mean," Ivy clarified, and Tate's eyes brightened.

"I love movies," Ivy confessed. She pulled some books out of her bag to hide how shy she felt. "I want to be a director someday." She glanced back up at Tate and saw that her eyes had widened.

"That. Is. So. Cool."

Ivy blushed. "Thanks."

"If you ever really do it, call me, okay? I would love to help make a movie."

Ivy couldn't suppress the grin that took over her face.

That afternoon, when Ivy rounded the corner on her way home from school, the police cars were parked in the driveway again. Her steps slowed but she didn't stop moving forward.

The doors of the second police car opened as she approached, and Ivy made a face. They seemed to already have a routine, the three of them. Her mom had a routine too. She stood on the steps with her feet planted and her arms crossed, scowling.

"What's going on now?" Ivy asked the policeman in the driver's seat.

"There's been an allegation that your mom may have been involved in removing merchandise from the QuickMarket."

"But she works at the QuickMarket."

The officer sighed, so softly Ivy almost couldn't hear him.

"What merchandise?" Ivy thought of the sack of flashlight batteries her mom had given her last week, and the popcorn. Also the half case of jam and the little pudding packets that had shown up in the kitchen one day.

The officer eased a blank expression over his face. "I'm afraid I can't say."

Really, Ivy didn't need him to say. If it was proof they were looking for, they'd find some right by her bed. She hadn't used any of the batteries at first when her mom handed them to her, she was still too angry about her notebook. But then, when her flashlight batteries died, she'd gone ahead and opened the packages. Despite everything, it had made her feel good that her mom remembered her like this, that she knew about her flashlight and had brought home something Ivy wanted and needed, and so much of it. She'd actually taken it as a sign that maybe life with her mom *could* get better. It never occurred to her the batteries might be stolen.

Her mom saw her and stretched her arm out. It was an order: *You come here.*

Ivy met her mother's gaze and asked with her eyes, *Did you do this?*

Her mother beckoned again. After half a second, Ivy turned and headed back down the walk.

"Hey, hold on—" the policeman called.

Ivy didn't.

"Ivy! Get back here. *Now,*" her mom yelled.

Ivy walked steadily onward.

She felt like one of Mom Evers's sewing pins trying to peel itself away from a big powerful magnet. (Ms. Mackenzie had brought magnets and pins in for their science section last week.) Her legs were as heavy as bags of cement. She'd helped Dad Evers with the addition's foundation before she moved, so she knew exactly how heavy that was: crazy heavy, much heavier than it seemed like one not-very-large sack of mortar could possibly be. Her feet were almost impossible to lift.

She did it, though. She put one foot in front of the other until she was halfway down the block. She risked a look over her shoulder then, but none of the policemen had followed her. Probably they had bigger fish to fry than one doomed girl. She turned the corner and kept walking.

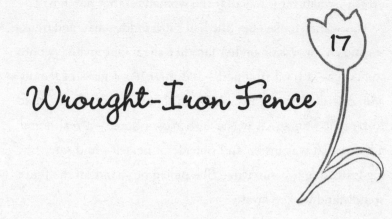

Wrought-Iron Fence

17

Ivy passed the pizza place and a park that was only a sliver of land between two houses. Two women pushed toddlers on the bucket-seat swings. After one glance, Ivy looked away. Aunt Connie used to take her to a park and push her on the swings when she was little. She was pretty sure her dad had too, though she only had wisps of memory about it.

She slowed down at the house with the wrought-iron fence. The woman who lived there was on the porch, reading in a wicker chaise, using Dad Evers's chair as an end table. She sipped from a red pottery mug and turned a page. Her face lit at whatever she'd read and it was like watching someone run into an old friend.

Ivy wrapped one hand around a fence spindle—the iron was cold, the grit of rust nibbled her palm—and gripped down until the spindle's edges creased her hand. She wanted—she *needed*—whatever it was that the woman on that porch had.

The woman looked up. She had short reddish hair and freckles and an expression on her face like she might invite Ivy onto the porch—a total stranger!—and offer her a glass of lemonade. A wish slashed through Ivy in that moment. She wanted to be that woman, at peace in her own home—a real home, a home that was inside and outside of herself—and safe. Living instead of just surviving. She pulled her hand off the fence spindle and walked away.

She passed the hospital and the school and kept going even though the neighborhood was less familiar. She went by a grungy-looking deli and a tattoo parlor and a dry cleaner with a HELP WANTED sign in the window. As much as she wanted to walk right out of her own life and into a new one, Ivy's steps began to slow. She heard shouting up ahead and slowed more.

Half a dozen boys were clustered in front of a bodega, jostling each other, talking loud. They called out rude things to two girls walking by and doubled over laughing when the girls grabbed each other's hands and ran.

Ivy gnawed on her thumbnail. Maybe if she waited they'd get bored and leave, or the bodega owner would chase them away. She turned and looked at the store she'd stopped in front of. A neon sign that said PAWN, BUY, SELL, INSTANT CA$H hung in the window.

Three electric guitars were propped on stands behind the glass. There was also an amplifier, a bowling ball, and a kitchen blender. The blender—chunky, with a yellow base—looked like the one Aunt Connie'd had. It had originally belonged to her mother, a grandmother Ivy didn't remember. She'd died when Ivy was tiny. Ivy hadn't seen her other grandma in so long she barely remembered her either. Because of what Ivy's mother had done, she didn't want anything to do with Ivy anymore.

Ivy moved on to the store's other window and saw something that made her heart skip a beat: a video camera with a price tag on it that said $350.

Ivy had wanted a video camera for as long as she could remember. She had a regular camera, one that had been Aunt Connie's, but it could only take about ten seconds of video, and then with only so-so resolution.

She put two fingers against the glass and imagined pushing the Record button. Then she let her hand fall again. She only had seventeen dollars to her name, and even if she had hundreds, what was the point? She was never going to get anywhere really, no matter what Ms. Mackenzie said. Look at how her life always went. The minute any good thing started happening, her mom came along like a storm to wreck it.

Ivy poked her lower lip out and started walking again.

Her face burned from what the boys in front of the bodega said to her, and her heart started to pound hard when two of them peeled off and followed her. She walked faster and so did they. The soles of her boots slapped the concrete; their feet echoed behind her. A bus shuddered up to the curb at the next corner, and Ivy raced to it.

"You got your pass?" the driver asked. She looked at him blankly.

He made a face and motioned her on with a jerk of his head.

The bus picked up speed after two more stops. Then the driver eased onto an entrance ramp and they were cruising south down Route 209. Ivy stared out the window at the fields and houses flashing by. Were they going to New York City? Someplace even farther away?

In one way, the idea of leaving was thrilling. But she had a spelling test in the morning and had the words down perfectly (*vacuous, vicarious, vindictive, vivacious, vitriol*), which hadn't been easy. Also she was hall monitor this week, a responsibility she didn't want to mess up. Besides all that, her mom was going to be furious. The threat of her mom's fury always hung in the air of their life, and thinking about it now made Ivy nervous.

She fiddled with her phone. Her finger hovered over Speed Dial. But she didn't want to have to explain things to the Everses: the police, her mom's work schedule. She turned the phone off and stuck it back in her pocket.

Higher Education

18

The bus turned off the highway and trundled through a village and kept going until they entered a college campus. Ivy gasped and pressed her nose against the glass.

She didn't know another kid her age who was as obsessed with the idea of college as she was. Even Prairie thought she was crazy to spend so much time worrying about getting in and getting scholarships. "Don't go nuts on me," she'd say if Ivy went on about it too much. "We're not even out of middle school yet."

That was easy for Prairie to say. It was fine if you wanted to be a goat farmer and knew it already, fine if you came from a family like hers, or just a family, period, one without a crater blasted in the middle of it.

The passengers started moving and Ivy followed. It dawned

on her now that they all looked like students: dreadlocks and a tie-dyed shirt on one, backpack with a laptop poking out of it on another, an enormous instrument case that had taken up a whole seat of its own with another. The boy with the instrument case grimaced at her. "Sorry to be so slow. Cello in motion. Hope I don't make you late."

The driver tapped her arm as she waited for the boy to maneuver the case down the steps. "Don't forget your pass next time. Rules are rules."

Ivy stared at him. He thought *she* was in college. That must be why he'd asked about her pass. It must be because of how tall she was, and the dress and the eye makeup. The driver began to frown and Ivy quickly smiled. "Okay," she said. "But the thing is, I have to get back—"

"I'm on another two hours. Just make sure you don't miss the six thirteen."

"Six thirteen. Got it. Thanks."

The driver winked. "Just like my granddaughter. She'd forget her own head if it wasn't attached."

"Right?" Ivy made her voice sound cheerful and—she hoped—carefree, but her legs were wobbly with relief.

Once she was off the bus, she wasn't sure what to do. She followed a tall, skinny girl up a set of steps and past a fountain and a building full of windows. The girl's steps were sure and quick and Ivy had to hurry to keep up. They jetted past more buildings and past a cart with a green-and-white-striped umbrella where a woman was selling sodas and juices. Ivy was thirsty but she didn't want to lose the girl, so she hurried onward.

She faltered when the girl swung toward a building with a sign that said it was a library. The girl disappeared inside and Ivy gazed after her. She wanted to stride in like the girl had, but she was afraid to. You'd almost certainly need a pass. Alarms might even go off if you didn't have one. Campus Security might come. She couldn't risk it. She turned to gaze over the campus.

There were flowering trees and students sprawled on the grass. A boy in a felt hat played a guitar; a girl in a flowing skirt sat beside him, singing. Her voice was scratchy and bold, and Ivy listened through two whole songs, until they picked up their things and walked off.

"—hope Hinson takes it easy on us, I never finished that section on succulents," Ivy heard the boy say.

"I know, it was crazy how long that was. Who knew there were so many kinds of cactus—wait, is it cactus or cacti when there's more than one—"

"Cactuses? Cactum?"

They laughed as they walked and then they were too far away to hear anymore.

The leaves of the tree beside Ivy rustled and the sweet smell of its blossoms was shaken out, like crumbs from a tablecloth. Ivy breathed deep. A thought appeared in her head like a message written on a billboard. She could be one of these students. She could stride into the library or sit on the lawn someday, no matter what her mother did. She *could*.

Ivy stood up. She had nearly two hours. She was going to investigate. She'd find the campus café and buy herself a cup of tea or maybe even a fancy coffee with the five-dollar bill she'd shoved in her pocket that morning, a habit she'd inherited from Aunt Connie, who never went anywhere, not even out in the yard to play badminton with Ivy, without some folding money in her pocket. She always said you never knew when you might need a little something, and Ivy thought now how right she had been.

Ivy found the student center and used the restroom, then browsed through the bookstore and bought three blue pencils that said *Ulster Senators* on them. Next she got into line at the café. "One ninety-nine," the girl at the register said when Ivy ordered tea.

Ivy paid and then stuffed her last dollar into a jar labeled *Tips*. The girl, who had shiny black hair and a silver ring in her eyebrow, grinned big.

Ivy pulled the tea toward herself. It was just the way she liked it, so hot that she had to be careful not to burn her lips or slosh it on her hands.

"Have a good day," the girl said.

Ivy shot a blinding smile at her. "I will," she said. "I am."

19

Oh Dear, Oh Dear

Ivy wandered to a kiosk plastered with flyers. A band called the Fiascos was playing on campus Saturday night and a motivational speaker was giving a talk on Wednesday. There were flyers about study groups, used textbooks, dances. Somebody was advertising himself as a handyman and someone else was looking for a housemate.

Ivy read that one again. Maybe the room was on the top floor of a house like the one with the iron fence. Maybe it had tall windows in deep frames, a window seat to read in. Ivy pictured herself unpacking a suitcase in a room with wooden floors, throwing her quilt from Mom Evers across the bed. She set her tea on the ground and ripped the number off and slipped the paper into her phone case where it couldn't get lost. Of course she couldn't call—she was only eleven!—but she liked the feeling taking the number gave her.

She was about to walk on again when she saw a flyer advertising an antique chicken feeder/waterer, complete with a picture. The feeder/waterer consisted of an old blue ball jar turned upside down into a tin tray that must've been made for that purpose. Once upon a time you must've been able to go to the general store and buy not only your flour and sugar and coffee and tea but also these little metal trays that would transform the jar you'd just emptied of spiced pears into a handy livestock feeder. Prairie would love it.

Whoever was selling the feeder was only asking ten dollars. Two of the little tabs were ripped off and Ivy ripped off another one, and then another, and then—this was probably really bad—she took the whole ad down and put it in her pocket. Maybe she could get it for Prairie for Christmas, or maybe just as a surprise, since Christmas was so far away still. Maybe it'd make up, a little, for lying about being sick. Her fingers were still curled around the paper when a voice said, "Hey!"

Ivy jumped and scrambled for an explanation for her theft. The nonscrambling part of her brain realized that the voice belonged to the boy from the theater.

Today he wore a dark blue T-shirt with a picture of the

White Rabbit on it. The rabbit wore a checkered jacket and carried an umbrella in the crook of his arm; he held a pocket watch in his paw and studied it anxiously. Ivy could almost hear him saying, *Oh dear, oh dear.*

The boy waved. "Hey! I keep seeing you everywhere."

Ivy's heart banged. She nodded.

He came up beside her. "What brings you way out in the boonies, anyway? Are you taking a class or something?"

Ivy shook her head.

"Just looking around?"

Ivy nodded again.

The boy nodded too, as if Ivy's being here, and her muteness, made perfect sense. "That's cool. Me, I'm here with my mom. She works here."

"Oh," Ivy managed to say.

"She's got me helping set up for this class she does every summer. Kind of a drag in one way—I have to cook dinner on her class nights. My dad is one hundred percent hopeless in the kitchen, so there's no counting on him to put food on the table." The boy smiled easily. "But it's cool. She does this intro to graphic novels every summer semester. I get to read all the books and student projects—" His smile became conspiratorial. "I only read the best ones, right? If I get bored, I just—" He sliced his hand in front of his throat.

Ivy felt a little smile slip out, despite how nervous she was.

"You like graphic novels?" he asked.

"I don't—know," Ivy croaked. She cleared her throat. "I like movies."

"Movies, *yeah*. But graphic novels are like movies, don't you think? The way they're written in frames? Or I guess they're more like comic books. Really good comic books."

Ivy attempted to look smart.

"I was thinking I might try to write one this summer. See how it goes."

"Uhn," Ivy said. She'd meant to say *yeah,* or *cool,* or at least *uh-huh,* but it hadn't come out right.

The boy pulled a heavy sheet of paper from his messenger bag, then a roll of packaging tape on a big dispenser. He held the poster up against the kiosk with one hand and applied the tape with four fast swipes. He moved around the kiosk and put up another poster, and then another. "But yeah, movies are cool. Obviously." He waved the tape dispenser at the flyers he'd hung. "Genetically predisposed to loving 'em, I guess. Family history of it and all that."

Ivy was about to ask what he meant when his attention shifted to a woman in a green blazer who was walking across the campus.

"There's my mom. I better go. See you." He waved his tape dispenser at Ivy.

"Bye," Ivy croaked.

He turned when he was twenty feet away. "I'm Jacob, by the way." He gave her a two-fingered salute and trotted off.

Ivy nodded at his vanishing back. "I'm Ivy," she said softly. "Ivy Blake."

He stopped again a moment later. "Oh, hey!" he called. "Almost forgot. Check out the poster!"

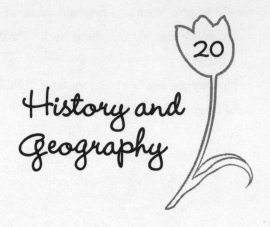

20

History and Geography

Ivy's mom flicked her eyes at Ivy when she walked in, then shifted them back to the TV. A game show was on. Bells rang; people cheered; her mom lifted a cigarette to her lips and then set it down again. "I missed work, I'll have you know. I don't know where I was supposed to start looking. I drove all around. I almost called the police to report you missing. I would've, in another hour."

"Sorry." Ivy went to the kitchen, found four thumbtacks in the drawer beside the sink, and headed to her room.

Her mom came to her door as she finished hanging Jacob's poster in the middle of her wall.

"What's that?"

"A poster." Ivy yanked *History and Geography* from her bag

and thwacked it onto her desk. Two of the stones from Skytop rattled to the floor.

"That thing's useless. I told you when you made it."

Ivy put the stones back next to her ivy plant, which Mom Evers had given her last year. *Your namesake,* she'd said. *Ivies are beautiful* and *strong. Adaptable.* Like her desk. She'd made it by laying an old door she'd found in the carport over two stacks of milk crates, and she was proud of it. It was shaky, but it worked. And it was gigantic. There was plenty of room to spread her stuff out, room for big pieces of paper (sometimes she cut grocery bags open and used them like canvases) and all her pencils and painting stuff.

Her mom drummed her fingers on the desktop; the tapping made a hollow sound. She traced a fingertip around the hole someone had made near the bottom—with a boot, probably. It was the right size and shape for that. Ivy scooted *History and Geography* over it.

"I should get you a real desk at the Goodwill next payday."

"No thanks." Ivy didn't bother to sound grateful even though a shiver went up her backbone. "I like this one."

Her mom moved closer and Ivy smelled Irish Spring. Tears pricked Ivy's eyes. The smell went with the memory of being cuddled on her mom's lap.

She squinted the tears away and pulled her *Go Math!* book and notebooks out of her bag. Then she pulled out the pencils she'd bought and lined them up alongside the books.

Her mom leaned over the bed. "So what's the poster about?"

"A film contest."

"A *film* contest?"

Ivy got an eraser out and set it carefully beside the pencils. "Yes."

"And is there some special reason we're hanging up a poster of a film contest like it's the *Mona*-freaking-*Lisa*?"

"I'm going to make a movie for it, I'm entering."

Her mom made a rude noise. "Make a movie with what? Your charm and good looks?"

"I guess so." Ivy gazed at her. "That plus the job I'm going to get."

"Job. Kid, let me tell you something. You're not going to find a job. I barely found a job, and I'm thirty, with a car and experience. Good luck."

"Thanks."

Her mother shook her head and turned to leave. Just before she went, she said, "I bought those batteries, for your information. In case you're thinking I took them."

Ivy raised her eyebrows at her mother's back.

"They were on sale because of going out of date, but I thought, heck, I'll bet they got some life left in them, I'll get them for Ives."

Ivy said, "Uh-huh."

Her mom turned to face her again. She didn't have any makeup on and her hair was damp. She must've taken a shower. She looked younger than usual. Softer, like the water had washed a shell away. "So you really think you can make a movie?"

"I know I can," Ivy said, although she didn't know any such thing.

"Well—good luck." This time it sounded like her mom really meant it.

Ivy frowned and sat down to read her chapter assignment in *History and Geography*. She didn't want to think about their own crazy history and all the strange, hard roads they'd bumped along.

The Answer to My Prayers

Ivy woke up thinking about the film contest. She flung her quilt back and sat down at her desk with a newly sharpened pencil and opened her journal to a fresh page.

JOBS, she printed at the top. She nibbled on her pencil eraser. It tasted smooth and surprisingly salty. Eventually she wrote *Dog walker.* Then, *Babysitter.* After that, *Lawn mower, House cleaner,* and *Dishwasher.* She'd seen how hectic it was through the swinging doors at the Really Fine Diner. Maybe they'd be desperate and hire someone underage. She nibbled on her eraser again. *Window washer, Papergirl, Gardener.*

With that, she slapped her notebook shut and went to the bathroom. She peered into the mirror as she brushed her teeth, trying to see if she looked different. She thought she did, around the eyes. More determined.

• • •

On the way to school she looked for a sign that anyone might need her to do anything. She passed the house she liked so much and wondered if the woman who lived there might need a gardener. But the lawn was mowed and the flower beds, though wild-looking, seemed to be in good order, so probably not.

At school she studied the bulletin board in the entryway and got excited when she saw the words *Attention, Babysitters!* at the top of one bright blue piece of paper. Then she saw the poster was advertising a babysitting *class*. She plodded off to Ms. Mackenzie's room, tugging on her braid.

"Earth to Ivy," Tate said when Ivy bumped into her on the way into room 203.

Ivy smiled at her distractedly.

"So I was wondering, do you want to go see a movie this weekend?"

Ivy blinked. "What?"

"A movie. Do you want to go see one? Saturday night, maybe? Or Sunday afternoon? My grandparents could take us, or my mom. We could pick you up."

Ivy imagined Tate seeing her house, meeting her mother. Her stomach clenched. Besides, she didn't want to—couldn't— miss spending the weekend with the Everses. "I, um. Yeah, it sounds fun. But—I don't know when I could."

A curtain eased over Tate's eyes. "Okay, sure. I get it." She started rummaging in her book bag.

Ivy yearned to make the curtain sweep back again. "It's just that I go away every weekend. But when summer vacation comes, then I probably could."

Tate quit sorting through her books. "Okay, then. It's a plan. Sort of a plan, anyway." She stuck her hand out and Ivy shook it firmly.

After school Ivy went into the dry cleaner on Broadway. The woman behind the counter guffawed when she asked about the HELP WANTED sign in the window. She actually slapped her leg, which Ivy'd never seen anyone do before. "Right. A schoolkid, that's the answer to my prayers."

Ivy slunk out. She almost didn't have the nerve to check the second place that had occurred to her, but she had to have that camera she'd seen in the pawnshop. She was going to do what she'd told her mom. She was going to get a job and enter that contest.

She pushed through the door into the dark, narrow deli. It had grimy floors that needed mopping.

"I'm looking for work," she told the man who leaned on the counter studying a newspaper.

The man wore pink-framed ladies' reading glasses and an apron that needed bleaching. He scratched the back of his head. "Man, oh, man, kid. I ain't really hiring."

Ivy frowned.

He looked apologetic. "Even if I was, I'd need someone during the day. Someone—you know—older. Not in school."

Ivy studied her boots. Sometimes it seemed like they were her only friends, these slightly too-large shoes that had traveled so far with her.

"Wouldn't be surprised if you wasn't a better worker than most of the adults I ever put on the payroll."

Ivy looked up sharply, but his face was regretful and closed.

At home Ivy fixed herself a hot dog and a can of beans and studied the help wanted ads in the newspaper she'd bought at the deli. She read each description carefully, turning it every direction in her mind to see if there was any way each job might fit her. It was like trying on clothes from the discount rack at the dollar store, and like those clothes, nothing was quite right. Nothing at all seemed like it would earn a kid three hundred and fifty dollars in a couple of weeks.

Helpful Henry

Saturday morning was sunny and warm. Ivy sat on the porch steps waiting for the Everses, her skirt bunched around her knees. When the station wagon rolled up, she called good-bye to her mom through the screen and trotted down the walk, her satchel bumping on her hip.

At the market grounds, Mom Evers squeezed the car in alongside Dad Evers's pickup loaded with chairs. There was just barely room to fit because of a truck on the opposite side that was straddling the dividing line. The passenger doors wouldn't open; Ivy had to climb out on Prairie's side.

Mom Evers opened the tailgate to reveal their eggs and the banana box full of supplies. "You two get your stuff set up and then help Dad with the chairs, okay? He's probably already got your table unloaded. I'll be there in a minute. I have to pee. *Again*."

Prairie made a face. "Mom. You don't say *pee* in front of people."

"Why not? You just did." They stuck their tongues out at each other and Ivy giggled. *This* was why she could never miss her weekends with them.

Prairie and Ivy each grabbed a box and headed for their spot in the pavilion. Their steps were matching: right, left, right, left. They glanced at each other, then put their arms around each other's shoulders and began flinging a leg over the other's leg with every step. It was tricky, like a dance step, only a more modern one than Grammy's box step. They had to be in perfect timing, each one pulling their leg out for another step at exactly the right moment so they wouldn't trip each other, but they were good at it. Of course. Ivy grinned. Prairie was magic. She *would* tell her, everything. Sometime today, she would find a time. She might even admit she hadn't really been sick last weekend.

When they got back to the car for another load, an old lady was dragging a case of jam from the back of the pickup that was blocking their car. Ivy watched, an idea niggling at her. When they came back the next time, the lady was slowly walking away from the truck with a box of jam clenched up against her chest.

Prairie grabbed a chair and headed back to the pavilion. Ivy tapped Dad Evers's arm. "Is it okay if I offer to help that lady? When we're done with the chairs?"

Dad Evers gave her one of his slow smiles. "Sure. Go on ahead right now. Prairie and I can finish these."

Ivy turned and took a breath, then trotted to catch up with the woman. "Um, ma'am? Can I help you do that?"

She ended up carrying box after box of jam, arranging the jars in pyramids on the old woman's table, which was right across the aisle from their own, and pointing all of their egg customers in that direction.

"Why are you being so nice to her?" Prairie whispered.

The lady wore a red ball cap and a bright green T-shirt, but the main thing you noticed about her was her giant frown. "How about you see to it that your kid's hands stay to himself!" she snapped at a woman who'd just bought three dozen eggs from the Everses and whose little boy had touched a jar of jam. The mother pulled the little boy close to her and hurried away.

Prairie shook her head. "You're going to make us look bad by association."

Ivy grimaced. She was embarrassed to admit she was hoping to earn some money for her efforts.

Toward the end of the day Ivy carted the remaining jam back to the lady's pickup, along with her heavy wooden lawn chair.

When the last box was loaded, she stood in front of the woman smiling. She tried to make the smile friendly, reliable, and humble all at the same time.

The woman pointed at the chair. "Fling that up there too, would you, since you're such a helpful Henry? Make sure you get it wedged in good so it don't flop around."

Ivy hefted the chair onto the tailgate and climbed up after it to push it to the front. She climbed back out and straightened her skirt.

"You ought to wear pants for work like this, not them dresses. Don't know what your ma was thinking."

Ivy kept smiling.

The old lady shuffled through her bag.

"Where'd I put those keys?" she muttered. Then with a *ha* of triumph she held up a ring of keys. She punched the fob and the truck's lights went on; its locks popped up with a unanimous *clunk*. She hauled herself into the driver's seat. "Take it easy, kid. Maybe I'll see you here next week, steer some of my customers your way. That jam of mine, it sells itself." She started up the truck and drove away.

Ivy let her foolish smile fade and trudged back to the pavilion.

"You seem quiet." Prairie handed Ivy the stack of empty egg cartons a man from High Falls had brought them. "Are you okay?"

Ivy put the cartons in the banana box, then lifted the table to start folding in the legs. Prairie lifted the other side at the exact same time and again Ivy wanted to tell her everything: her mom's new work schedule, the police cars, the film contest, all of it.

They lugged the table to the pickup and started back to the stall.

"So, um," Ivy said as Prairie's cell phone rang. It sounded like a tinny player piano and Ivy lost her step. When they got the phones they'd both set them with an old-fashioned land-line ring and Ivy wouldn't have dreamed of changing hers. Prairie dropped her arm from Ivy's shoulder and pulled her phone out. "Hi!"

Ivy started walking again and kept her eyes on the ground, like there was something fascinating there.

"No, I can't, I have company. That doesn't work."

"No." Pause. "No." Then a laugh. Ivy walked faster. Prairie hurried to catch up.

At the stall, Ivy refolded their tablecloth into a tighter square.

"No, I'll call you when I know." Prairie stared across the emptying market ground; she squinted like she was gazing across a wide-open plain. "Sunday night, maybe. That'd prob-ably work." She ended the call and shoved her phone in her pocket.

"Sorry. We're doing this project for 4-H—a breeding program, only just on paper—and that was Kelly, wanting to talk about it. So anyway—you seem quiet, are you okay?"

"Yeah, I'm fine."

"I still wish you were doing 4-H." Prairie took aim at a pebble and gave it a whap with the side of her foot. "Nothing's as fun without you."

Ivy's feelings shifted again. She *would* tell Prairie—

There was a sound behind them, a groan. Mom Evers had come back from the port-a-potties at the edge of the market. She sank into a chair that hadn't been packed yet, holding her stomach with both hands like it was a vase that had almost fallen off a shelf. Her face was pale.

"Prairie, go get your dad."

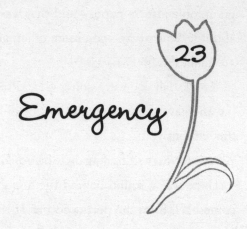

Emergency

It was an hour before Dad Evers came back out into the emergency room's waiting area. He squatted in front of them. "They're okay. Mom and the baby both."

Ivy's shoulders relaxed, finally. She took a deep breath and exhaled it slowly. The best part of her day—week, month, *year*—bloomed in her head like it was scrawled in neon: *this moment*, the moment she knew Mom Evers and the baby were okay.

"Ordinary spotting, the doc said. Nothing to worry too much about, though she's supposed to take it easy, the next while, till the baby comes."

Prairie touched his shoulder; he pushed a lock of hair behind her ear.

Ivy wanted to reach out or say something too, but she

couldn't. She'd been struck mute ever since Mom Evers told Prairie to get Dad Evers.

"Half hour or so, we can go. I'm going to try and get the bill figured out. Prairie, you'd better call Grammy. She'll be climbing the walls."

Ivy picked up a *National Geographic*. She opened it and tried to let the trouble in the emergency room swirl around her without noticing it too much. There was a sweating girl who seemed delirious, a woman with what looked like a broken arm, and a man whose skin was as gray as floor paint. It all made Ivy feel nauseous, and that made her mad at herself.

She turned pages slowly. In the magazine, young people stood on a windswept rock in Iceland. A cowboy squatted by a campfire. The photos were interesting, but Ivy couldn't concentrate. She was about to set the magazine down when a voice sliced into her haze.

"But how'm I going to get my house cleaned with my leg in a cast?" a woman cried. She sat in a wheelchair, staring at the receptionist. Her hair was dyed black and her lipstick was a red slash across her mouth. She'd put too light a face powder on, and her eyes were wide and peering. "How am I?"

"I don't know, ma'am."

The woman leaned forward. "Caroline, my daughter, she's coming to visit in June. I have to have the house cleaned, or she won't like it. She'll think I can't stay on my own any longer."

Ivy's heart tightened in sympathy.

"Well, you'll have to hire some help, I guess. Do you want me to call you a taxi, or is there someone who'll come pick you up?"

"No, there's no one to pick me up! I *told* them not to bring me to a hospital so far away because there's no one to help. That's what I'm saying, don't you see?"

Ivy could tell that the receptionist did not see. She wasn't really paying attention. Ivy couldn't exactly blame her. The emergency room was crowded; the girl who seemed delirious was now crying. The receptionist sat like her back hurt and had dark circles under her eyes. Maybe she had a new baby at home and the baby kept her up nights, or maybe it was even more interesting than that—

Ivy made herself stop. The point was that this problem had already been solved as far as the receptionist was concerned: one busted femur, set, cast, checked out, and billed, *next*.

But for the old lady, the problems were just starting.

Ivy slid off her seat and walked to the woman's wheelchair. "I could help you," she said. "If you could pay me."

Up a Tree

Ivy and Prairie swung their legs over the edge of their tree house late that evening. Ivy stared at Fiddle the rooster's red comb and listened to the silence vibrate. She'd barely been able to convince Prairie to come out here. "I have something to tell you," she finally said.

"Well?" Prairie stared straight ahead; her fingers were tight on the tree house platform.

"I wanted to tell you why I told Mrs. Grizzby I'd help her if she'd pay—"

Prairie's head snapped around; her expression made Ivy's heart hurt. "I can't believe you did that. Is it your mom or something? Did she change her mind about letting you go on our trip and you just didn't know how to tell me?"

"It's not my mom."

The air in the branches of the maple seemed to hold its breath.

"Not your mom."

Ivy mashed her thumb against a maple seed. "It is kind of my mom, but not the way you think. It's really me. There's something I have to do. The thing is, I want to make a movie."

"Make a movie."

Prairie's voice was flat and the words gave Ivy a mean little shove, just like when her mom said them. Ivy slogged on. "Yes. It's my dream, you know that, and I need a camera—"

"But you don't have to suddenly take some job that starts the minute school gets out, do you? I mean, really? There's no other time?"

"No. It has to be now."

Prairie narrowed her eyes. "Why?"

Ivy flexed her toes inside her boots. She had been wearing these boots when Ms. Mackenzie told her to never give up. She had been wearing them when the police showed up, and when she walked away from them and her mom. She thought of the policemen's shiny oxfords and the look in their eyes. It was all complicated, but she had to figure out a way to make Prairie see.

She tried to make her mouth form the words to explain, but she wanted to go to North Carolina so badly. She wanted to take the train from Poughkeepsie to Greensboro and then the bus to Asheville, and from there ride in Grammy's friend Dorothy Peacock's lemon-yellow Cadillac Eldorado convertible car all the rest of the way to Vine's Cove, where Grammy'd grown up and where Great-Uncle Tecumseh still lived.

Prairie had told her approximately one million times in the past year how Great-Uncle Tecumseh lived in a little cabin made of pine logs and plank floors, and how when you woke up in the morning the first thing you heard was the sound of the breeze whispering through the trees and the burble of Vine's Creek tumbling down the mountain, and the song of a cardinal, maybe. She said that at night owls hooted and coyotes howled, and that every day the two of them would tromp all over Vine's Cove, up and down the mountainside, exploring. She was going to take Ivy to the ruins of a settler's cabin and to a place deep in the woods where there were the remains of an old still. For making whiskey! She said they'd fish in the creek and help in the garden and every night they'd sit around the campfire Great-Uncle Tecumseh built, and that for two whole weeks it would be like they had traveled to some far-off country that most people never even dreamed existed.

Ivy wanted to see it all, hear it all, smell it all. She wanted it more than anything. Except this.

She sucked in another breath. "It's kind of a long story." Her voice wavered. "But the truth is, it hasn't been all that great with my mom. It's been really hard and I need—I don't know. I need to do something for myself, and this job is my chance."

• • •

Prairie tapped her thumb on her leg while Ivy talked.

When she finished, Prairie studied her with one eye squeezed shut, like Ivy was a fence post that wouldn't stand straight. "I'm really sorry it hasn't been great with your mom. I get that you want to make a movie too, but what's so important about this exact contest and this one job? This is our *trip*. It's our vacation. We've been looking forward to it forever. I thought you really wanted to go."

"I do."

Prairie kicked at the air. "It doesn't seem like it. It sure does not."

"I do want to. But this other thing, the movie—it can't wait." Ivy couldn't even try to explain how it all hinged together—the police, tearing herself away from her mom's command, walking and walking until she stopped at the pawnshop, seeing the camera, and then meeting Jacob on the campus and realizing that making the movie—and even maybe, hopefully, winning the contest—was the key to everything. It was *symbolic*. She squeezed her hands into fists and poured all her concentration into the hope that Prairie would understand this the way she did so many things. "The job is now, and I need the camera. And if I don't do it, if I don't do *some*thing, I'll be—a nothing. Like my mom."

"No you won't! That's dumb. That's probably the dumbest thing you ever said."

Ivy made herself smile because she knew Prairie meant this as a compliment. She wished Prairie would've added another sentence or two, though. *Your mom is not a nothing. In spite of everything, she isn't.* Something like that. Even though Ivy was furious at her mom most of the time these days, she did wish that. She wished other people saw the good side of her mom the way she did. An image from a long time ago of her mom tickling Aunt Connie and both of them giggling flashed in her head. Then one of sitting beside her mom on the couch watching television, their hands bumping inside the popcorn bag.

Prairie hiked her knee up and wiped an invisible smudge off the toe of one boot. She almost always wore her boots, leather Red Wings like Dad Evers's, no matter what the weather was or where she was going or what else she had on, even a dress, until summer came. Then she went barefoot every minute she could and never seemed to mind how dirty her feet got.

Ivy loved that. She loved how Prairie was a whole piece of fabric. Ivy was not. Instead there was a hole in the middle of her, a big, ragged tear she could feel ripping bigger all the time. Doing this movie—it was to mend that hole. It would be a matter of sewing herself together, darning herself up the best she could. She picked at a piece of lichen.

"How come you can't come to North Carolina and make a movie? There's lots of cool stuff to film there. Uncle Tecumseh could tell you stories—"

"I need a camera first." Ivy put big spaces between the

words so that Prairie would get the point. "I have to have three hundred dollars. Three hundred and fifty plus tax, actually. I can earn it working for Mrs. Grizzby." When the lady with the broken leg introduced herself as Inez Grizzby, Ivy had felt even more sorry for her.

"Maybe Mom and Dad could lend it to you."

"No."

"Grammy, then—"

"*No*. That won't work." None of the Everses could afford to loan her money, and besides, she needed to do this by herself.

Prairie kicked at the air again. "So you're really going to make a movie?"

"Yes."

"You really think you can?"

"I do think so. I can. I will."

The chickens ambled below them, pecking at bugs. Fiddle stretched his wings out bossily. He flapped at a hen to make her move—he'd found something he wanted her to eat—and the hen squawked in irritation but then went where Fiddle wanted. Ivy smiled sadly. She loved the chickens. Not as much as Prairie did, but she did love them. And this day, sitting here in the tree house saying a hard, sad thing and staring down at the flock below, was almost exactly like the day she'd told Prairie what had happened between her mom and dad.

She'd been so frightened then. Frightened that Prairie would draw back in horror. That she wouldn't want to be friends any longer.

She was almost as frightened now. But Prairie wouldn't disappoint her. Ivy turned to explain even better—she'd skimmed over the hardest parts pretty fast—but Prairie got up onto her knees and scrambled down the ladder.

Hate

Ivy went to bed early that night. She didn't know what else to do. Prairie was snuggled on one end of the couch with a book when Ivy got inside and wouldn't meet Ivy's eye, and suddenly the farmhouse didn't seem as much like home as usual.

In the morning Ivy pretended not to wake up when Prairie climbed out of the top bunk. When she was sure Prairie wasn't coming back, she crept to the stairs. She sat there alone. Pup hadn't even come with her.

Prairie's voice wafted up from the kitchen along with the smell of pancakes. "It's like she's not even the same person."

Ivy heard the scrape of a spatula, then a soft *flop*. Mom Evers, flipping the cakes up in the air the way she did, then catching them and easing them back onto the griddle.

"Everything changes, sweetie. And everyone's entitled to change."

"Well, I don't like it."

Mom Evers made a sound that was half a laugh. Someone scraped a chair back and the kitchen door opened and shut. Dad Evers. He wouldn't want to listen to this. He'd go outside and sand chairs instead. Ivy wished she could go with him. She wouldn't want to talk, either. She'd just sit and watch him work. She hugged her knees.

"I can't believe she asked that old lady for a job that's right during our trip. And when you were in the hospital, too. Something might've happened to you! Something might've happened to the baby."

"Well, but I was okay, sweetie. The baby and I are fine. We're okay, and Ivy knew that when she asked, you told me already. Don't be mad at her for that."

"I am, though. I *am* mad at her, I can't help it."

Mom Evers made the sound again.

"Aren't you?"

"Aren't I what? Mad at Ivy?"

"Yeah."

"No. Not mad. Sad for her, is more it."

Ivy balled her fists up.

"But she's so different. I never thought she could be like this. She's almost—cold. Like her mom, sort of."

"Oh, I don't think that. I think she has a lot going on and a lot to figure out and she's trying to sort through it all."

"But without us!"

"Well, maybe. Maybe she has to pull away to see things clearly. Maybe we have to let her."

"I *hate* it," Prairie cried.

Ivy wanted to go smashing down the stairs and tell Prairie she hated it too. Hated being talked about and misunderstood, hated having to lie sometimes, hated having a mission that she had to undertake instead of going to North Carolina and having a good time, and, maybe most of all, hated being pitied.

She clasped her arms around her knees and leaned forward, straining to hear what Grammy would say.

The teakettle whistled, a cupboard door opened, a spoon clunked inside a cup. Grammy, stirring sugar into her tea. Ivy knew the sound as well as she knew which mug Grammy would've taken, the pale blue one with dimpled squares all around its outside and a milky-white interior. A minute later a chair scraped again: Grammy sitting back down.

Ivy waited, hardly breathing. There was quiet until Prairie said, "She doesn't even get why I don't want just the chickens anymore. But you can't make a living on just chickens, and besides that, they don't lay forever. You have to slaughter them or else wait for them to die, and I hate that."

"There's a lot of hate spouting out of you for so early in the morning." Grammy sounded tired. "You might want to taste your words before you get in such a yank to spit them out."

"Grammy!"

"Just saying."

There was a space of quiet before Prairie spoke again.

"Goats live longer. And dairy goats you don't have to really think about as meat at all, you know? Kelly thinks LaManchas are the best for cheese, but I think Saanen. LaManchas don't give enough every day, you'd never make anything. We keep arguing about it. Kelly says it doesn't matter, it's only on paper, but it *does* matter. It matters to me."

"Kelly's pretty opinionated, isn't he?" Mom asked in a smiling voice, and Ivy sat poleaxed. This Kelly person was a *boy*.

"Saanens *are* better. It's just obvious. They're so big and sweet *and* they produce the most milk. Anybody with half a brain could see it."

Mom Evers laughed. Then she said, "I think you need to take it easy on Ivy. Moving is hard. Getting used to a new school, living with her mom again—cut her some slack."

Prairie sighed. "It's just—I miss her. And it feels like she doesn't miss us."

"She misses us."

Ivy shivered with how much she did miss the Everses and with how essential it was that she never let them know how much. If they knew that, they'd also know how bad things were with her mom.

"Walk a mile in her moccasins," Grammy said. "Put yourself in her boots, see what the view's like. As advice goes, it's an oldie but a goodie."

Prairie made a noise, an *augh* of frustration that was so familiar Ivy almost wanted to smile.

Then Prairie said, "Fine! I'll try!" in a pretend-mad voice and Grammy chuckled and Dad Evers came in saying, "What's all this hilarity?"

Ivy shoved her fists under her armpits. She felt like a lizard was turning around and around in her stomach, scraping up different feelings with every turn: anger, sadness, shame, and then anger again. That part surprised her, but she hated hearing herself discussed like this.

"I-vee! Breakfast!" Grammy called up the stairs. Ivy stood just as Grammy poked her head around the corner. "Oh, there you are. It's time to eat, Knasgowa. It's pancakes, your favorite."

Ivy smiled at her grimly. "Thanks, Grammy, but I'm not hungry. I think maybe I'll go home early, if somebody can take me."

Grammy frowned. "That doesn't sound like you—"

"I'm not feeling very good. My stomach hurts."

Grammy climbed the steps and put the back of her hand against Ivy's forehead. Ivy closed her eyes and let herself pretend for one more moment that she really could belong here, inside this family instead of always just at the edge of it. "You do feel a little warm."

"My throat hurts too." It was true. Ivy felt strangled by a rope of anger braided with grief.

401 Elderberry

The Monday after school let out, Ivy pushed her bike from under the carport at eight a.m. She swung a leg over her bike bar and coasted onto the street. It was sunny and birds were singing cheerfully, but Ivy was miserable. When a robin aimed a snippet of melody at her, she glowered at it. Then she reminded herself that her misery was not the robin's fault. It was her own doing. *She* had chosen not to go to North Carolina. Even her mom had tried to talk her into changing her mind last night.

She pictured Prairie and Grammy on the train as she turned onto Broadway. Their eyes would be bright, they'd be leaning forward in their seats. Prairie would have on her red cowboy shirt with the pearly buttons. Grammy, who didn't care about clothes at all, would have on the green velvet tracksuit she'd ordered out of a catalogue especially for the trip. She'd have a sack of peppermints in her purse; she'd take one and then offer one to Prairie as the sights flashed by their window and the train clattered south to the city.

Ivy leaned over the handlebars and pumped the pedals hard. Her expression was so forbidding that a dog who'd been thinking of darting out and snapping at her ankles decided to stay on his porch.

Half an hour later, Ivy coasted up to the address Mrs. Grizzby had given her: 401 Elderberry loomed over the street. It was built of red bricks that were crumbling at the corners and had a chimney with a chunk missing out of its top. The shutters needed paint, the porch had two broken columns, and a porch swing creaked lonesomely on its chains.

Ivy perched on her bike seat with her toes on the ground, staring. If she was smart, she'd turn right around and go home. She made a face and cruised up the driveway.

On the porch she stood before a dark green door with a brass handle that had a design of vines and leaves etched into it. A radio played from somewhere deep in the house. Ivy breathed in shallowly. There was a sour smell, an oldness that seemed to rise from the earth beneath the place. She tugged on her braid. Then she squared her shoulders and jabbed the doorbell button.

A clumping sound came slowly nearer. Eventually the door opened and Mrs. Grizzby appeared, propped on crutches.

Ivy smiled at her.

Mrs Grizzby frowned like Ivy was a stain on the carpet, except that Ivy could already tell there was no way you'd ever be able to see her carpets. The room the door opened into was filled with boxes and piles and mounds and stacks of stuff. A stairway led to the second floor, and every step had so much stuff on it so that you'd hardly be able to fit your foot on the tread.

Ivy smiled wider. "Hi! It's me. Ivy. Come to help you clean."

"But why are you wearing *that*? I thought you'd come to *work*."

Ivy had spent a long time choosing her outfit that morning: a denim jumper over a plain white T-shirt. Nice but not fancy. Practical but respectful. "I have, for sure, that's why—"

"You can't clean in that!"

The train had pulled out of the station not fifteen minutes ago. Staying for this job *had* to be worth it. "Yes, I can," she said quickly. "It's just old stuff from the thrift shop. Or I can go home and change if you want—"

Mrs. Grizzby shook her head as if this was a showstopping problem and nothing Ivy said could fix it. Then she said peevishly, "Oh, come in, I guess."

Cat Vomit and Dragon Fruit

Two weeks later, Ivy knelt on the stair runner with a bottle of upholstery cleaner. She scrubbed while Mrs. Grizzby watched from below.

"You missed a spot! Over there, to the right."

Ivy scrubbed harder at what might've been a patch of ancient cat vomit.

"Not too hard! You'll rub the color out."

Ivy kept scrubbing at the same rate as before. Mrs. Grizzby wasn't as aggravated as she sounded most of the time. She was just—nervous. She had a prickly, strange-looking outside and a sweet, tender center, like some exotic fruit from the bodega. A dragon fruit, maybe, or an African horned cucumber.

Ivy had learned that a few days after she started. She had taken a framed photo of a man down from the mantel to clean, and asked who it was. Mrs. Grizzby clapped her hands together; her eyes sparkled and her face glowed. Ivy gaped at her, she was so surprised by the change.

"Why, that's my husband. That's Charlie." Mrs. Grizzby took the photo and wiped the glass off with her sweater sleeve. "We met in college. He was in my economics class. He was *very* good-looking."

She winked at Ivy and Ivy couldn't help but grin in return. She had taken the photo of the ordinary-looking man out of Mrs. Grizzby's hands and cleared all the junk surrounding it, and filed away this new information about her employer: she wasn't just an odd, difficult old lady who wore too much makeup. She was a *person*. She was real.

It was hard to remember all the time, like when Mrs. Grizzby hovered over her insisting Ivy be careful with a box of old pickle jars that were never going to be used for anything.

"There's another spot, right under your hand," Mrs. Grizzby cried now, like the spot was on fire. Ivy moved her hand and bore down on it.

"It really looks nice." Mrs. Grizzby tapped the armrest of her wheelchair in a contented way late that afternoon. They were at the kitchen table with tiny quilted canning jars of soda in front of them. Mrs. Grizzby had insisted she had to keep the glasses because they'd come full of jelly in a fruit basket from Caroline at Christmas twelve years before. She said the flavors were strawberry, raspberry, and blackberry, and they had been good, except a little seedy. Also the oranges had been a little dry and the apples not so crisp, but the basket itself had been nice; she still had it somewhere—

Ivy had quit arguing and put the jars back in the cupboard instead of hauling them to the recycling bins out on the curb. The bins had never had anything in them before; Ivy'd had to run out to the street and flag the city truck down to get them emptied.

"It hasn't looked so nice in years. Caroline's going to like it so much. I'll bet she ends up staying a whole week." Mrs. Grizzby hugged herself. "Oh, we'll have such a good time."

"Mmm." Ivy stirred her ice cubes with her finger so she'd have somewhere to look. The phone had never rung while she was there. No letters or postcards had dropped into the iron box by the door, and in all the stacks of old mail and newspapers that were piled on the table beside Mrs. Grizzby's chair, there had been only three things from Caroline: a Christmas card, an Easter card, and a Mother's Day greeting. All of them had just her name signed under the preprinted messages.

"Don't you think so?" Worry flowed back over Mrs. Grizzby's face.

"Oh! Yes! Of course. I'll bet she will. Maybe she'll even want to stay *two* weeks."

"You really think so?"

Ivy nodded and lifted her jelly-jar glass in a toast and downed her four ounces of soda.

Canon GL1 MiniDV 3CCD

Ivy handed the crumpled twenties Mrs. Grizzby had given her to the man behind the pawnshop's counter. Her heart banged hard as he counted the money. The job with Mrs. Grizzby was done; it'd be hard to get so much money at once again. What if she was spending it wrong? What if the whole idea was dumb? She opened her mouth to say *Wait,* but the man was already shoving the drawer shut. He swaddled the camera in bubble wrap and poked it into a box that had once held Wint O Green Life Savers. He pushed the box and her change across the counter. "It's all yours."

Ivy drew the box close. The minute she wrapped her arms around it, her doubts evaporated.

She stood up straighter and waited for the man to congratulate her. This camera was something a film student in college might use. A guy who made TV commercials had raved about it online; an independent filmmaker said she'd shot her movie with a camera like this.

But the man just stabbed his copy of her receipt on a spindle by the register. "Enjoy." He looked over her shoulder at the next customer, a skinny man in a sleeveless T-shirt cradling the kitchen blender.

Ivy began pedaling toward home, the camera box jammed into her book bag. It was heavy and bumped into her back every time she hit her left pedal, but she didn't mind that. She did mind that she'd coast in under the carport at home and jiggle the front door lock and set the box on the couch and open it, all alone, and that would be that.

She thought of Jacob saying, *Movies, yeah.* He'd have understood how momentous this was. Too bad there was no way to find him. There was no way to find anyone. Prairie and Grammy were on a train somewhere in Maryland, if Ivy'd been keeping track right, and Mom and Dad Evers were in New Paltz, and busy.

Ivy pumped her bike pedals around a few more times. Then, without planning it, she took a right turn rather than a left at the corner of Broadway and Elm and headed across town.

"But what'll you *do* with it?" Mrs. Grizzby's mouth was turned down in puzzlement.

The candles Ivy had put out on the dining room table in holders she found in the back of a cupboard were almost out of sight behind a mound of newspapers. Ivy had hauled all the newspapers to the recycling bin right before she left, but Mrs. Grizzby must've limped outside on her crutches and somehow hauled them back in. Mrs. Grizzby put one hand on top of them, like she could hide them that way. "What story will you tell? Who'll be the actors and all that?"

Ivy stared at her.

"Will you take a class, or get books from the library to figure it all out, or what?"

Ivy tugged her braid. Then she said, "Yes, I'll get books," like she'd thought of that already. "And I know a boy who loves movies who might be able to tell me some stuff about making one."

Mrs. Grizzby raised her penciled brows.

"Plus, my friend Tate from school wants to help."

Mrs. Grizzby's face didn't lose its doubtful, waiting look.

"And I'll just, sort of, figure it out."

"I see." Mrs. Grizzby gnawed on her dark red lip. Ivy had a feeling she *did* see. She saw that Ivy didn't have a clue what she was doing. They gazed at the camera. Its label said *Canon GL1 MiniDV 3CCD Camcorder Pro Digital Video Camera.* Mrs. Grizzby tapped the words cautiously. "How do you even turn it on?"

Ivy didn't know. She rebundled the camera in the bubble

wrap and set it back in the box. She smiled brightly. "I'm sure there are directions. I'll have to read them and find out. Anyway, I better get home now."

Mrs. Grizzby's shoulders slumped.

Ivy stopped tucking the box's flaps under each other. "I guess I'll—see you sometime? If you ever need help with cleaning or anything, call me, okay?"

Mrs. Grizzby frowned. "Cleaning? I don't need help with cleaning. It's only because of Caroline coming that I had you help straighten things up a little. I could've done it all myself if it wasn't for this darned cast, and the crutches and chair and all."

"Oh, sure." Ivy froze her smile in place so it wouldn't look skeptical. "I know." She picked up her camera box. "Well, good-bye, I guess, then."

Mrs. Grizzby followed her to the door, her crutches thumping. She patted Ivy's shoulder before Ivy stepped out onto the porch. "Good luck with that fancy-pants camera. Call me if you ever need an old lady in one of your movies." She smiled that sudden, real smile, and Ivy impulsively wrapped her arms around her waist before she ran down the steps.

At home, Ivy put her camera box on her desk. She listened to the sounds the house made: a fan her mom had left running in her bedroom whirred; water from the kitchen faucet plopped into the basin. Ivy sighed, then dug the instructions from the box and began to read.

A few hours later she'd filmed everything in the house. Another hour after that, she'd documented Mrs. Phillips pulling crabgrass from her petunia bed. Her feeling of excitement grew. When Mrs. Phillips said she was tired of weeding, Ivy ran back inside and found Tate's phone number. Ivy had asked her for it on the last day of school.

No one answered, but Ivy left a message. "So, um, hi. It's Ivy—Ivy Blake, from school—calling for Tate. I wanted to tell you, I got my camera today! Well—you didn't know about that, but I finally earned enough money for it. And now I'm figuring out how to use it and pretty soon I'm going to start working on a movie. I kind of hoped—you said if I ever made a movie— well, that you'd want to help. So I wanted to tell you. And see if you wanted to get together or something. Sometime. Yeah, so that's all. Bye!"

Ivy slammed the phone down, her face warm with shyness. Then she ran back outside and started filming her walk to school, past the tiny park and the tattoo parlor and the pizza place. She adjusted the focus to get a sharper view of a postal box. Everything in the world suddenly seemed interesting and beautiful and new, like she'd never seen any of it before.

29

As Good as It Gets

Ivy cruised up to her house on her bike one muggy afternoon, her book bag pulling at her shoulder, and frowned when she saw the Mustang in the drive. She jiggled the key in the lock and slipped inside. There was a sound of chopping from the kitchen. Water ran and a pot banged on a stove burner. Something crashed to the floor and her mom said *dang* softly, the way you said things to yourself when you thought you were alone. Ivy tugged on her braid and headed for the kitchen.

She opened her eyes wide when she got there, like she hadn't noticed the car outside. "Mom! I thought you had to work." Her mom's boss had kept her on even after she'd had the police come. She'd said she knew Ivy's mom had a child to support, and that she'd let it go as long as it never happened again. That had made her mom mad because nothing *had* happened as far as she was concerned. She'd only done what Lindsey told her was okay to do.

"Yeah, well. Not today."

Her mother stood looking down into a pot; the room smelled of boiling potatoes. Ivy poured herself a glass of tea, added ice cubes, and took a tentative sip as if the amount of ice compared to tea was the only thing on her mind. "How come?"

Her mom didn't answer and Ivy went back to the chair where she'd dropped her bag. She began stacking books on the table: *Making Movies, Filmmaking for Teens, The Hero's Journey.*

"What's all that?"

"Books." Ivy had spent the afternoon at the library. Mrs. Grizzby was right. It wasn't so easy to figure out how to make a movie.

"It's summer vacation and you still can't get enough of books?"

"Nope." Ivy smiled to take the shortness out of her answer.

Her mom leafed through *The Hero's Journey,* then went back to the first page. "'There are only two or three human stories,'" she read. Ivy took a sip of her tea as her mom finished the quote: "'and they go on repeating themselves as fiercely as if they had never happened before.'"

Ivy studied her mom from behind the safety of her tea glass. If there were only a few human stories, she wondered why her mom had to star in such a sad one. And whether her own had to be the same. Ms. Mackenzie had said no. Ivy hoped she was right.

Her mother put her finger on the line of text. "Willa Cather. Sounds like catheter."

"She's a famous writer, Mom."

"Famous, huh? Is that what you want to be? Famous?"

Ivy ran her thumb up and down the sweaty outside of her tea glass. Nothing she said would be right, but the answer was no. Famous wasn't the point.

Her mother picked up *Making Movies* and riffled the pages so fast that Ivy was afraid she'd tear them. "Pretty swanky stuff there, Ives. Isn't it too old for you?"

"It's just a book, Mom."

Her mother took *Filmmaking for Teens* off the stack. She flipped through a few pages and then let it fall closed too. "You're not exactly a teen yet."

Ivy shrugged one shoulder. She pretty often felt a hundred years older than she was. That was part of the reason she loved Prairie so much. With Prairie, she felt like a regular eleven-year-old kid. Or maybe it was that with Prairie, it seemed okay to be whatever she was. Ivy missed her with a sudden hard pang.

"So how come you haven't been on the phone with the great girlfriend since she got back from down south?"

Ivy glanced up sharply at her mom. She could go for ages without seeming like she was paying any attention to Ivy at all, and then zip in like a hawk on her exact thoughts. "I don't know."

"What about the farmers' market? I notice you didn't go last Saturday."

Ivy shrugged. The phone had rung on Friday while her mom was at work, and for reasons Ivy didn't completely understand, she'd let the answering machine get it. It had been Prairie. Ivy hadn't picked up, and Prairie hadn't called back. Yet.

"She dump you, that what it is?"

"No!"

"You get tired of her?"

"*No.* She's my best friend."

"You don't act like it lately."

"Well, she *is.*" Ivy thought of the postcards tucked into her sketchbook, mountain scenes from North Carolina, all of them a little faded. They'd been coming in the mail all week; every one had been the best part of Ivy's day. Ivy could imagine Prairie taking them out of a dusty rack in a far corner of the Vine's Cove General Store, and grinning to herself as she wrote the messages.

The first two had come on the same day. SO MAD, was written in Prairie's firm printing on one. In the bottom right corner, in small letters, she'd written 3/6. The other card said, LOVE, PRAIRIE. The numbers on that one were 6/6. The next day a card that said, I GOT arrived, with a 2/6 in the corner, and the day after that the message read, WERE HERE (5/6).

Then there was nothing until yesterday when there'd been one more. WISH YOU, it said, and 4/6.

Ivy wished too. She wished everything was simpler. She wished she didn't have so much to hide and that she wasn't so mad deep inside over what she'd heard the Everses say. That they were sad for her. That she needed to be cut some slack.

On the stove, the potato water boiled high and lifted the pot lid. Foam cascaded over the edge of the kettle and hissed onto the burner. Her mom whipped around and yanked the lid off. She yelped as the steam burned her wrist.

"Are you all right?"

Her mom held her wrist under the tap. She looked exhausted suddenly and Ivy's heart went soft. Her mom turned the tap off and studied her wrist, then peered into the kettle and shook it slightly. "I was going to make mashed potatoes for supper, but not now I guess. They're all stuck to the bottom."

"It's all right. We can use the good parts."

Her mom made a sound that wasn't quite a laugh. "Scraping off the burnt parts. That's about as good as it gets for people like us."

Ivy began scooping unburned potatoes into a bowl. "How come you're not at work?"

Her mother's shoulders sagged. "I got fired today. The boss still thinks I'm stealing, which is bull. I never stole anything."

Ivy nodded. Her mom was a lot of things, but a thief had

never been one of them. She probably *hadn't* taken the batteries. They probably had been on sale. They were almost expired, after all.

"I worked hard at that station. I was never late, I never took off early, I never slacked around like Lindsey does."

Ivy gave her mom a sympathetic look. Her mom did always take pride in being a good employee even when she hated her jobs. It was one of those surprising things about her, like making her bed.

"I think Lindsey set me up."

Ivy's eyes went wide. "How?"

"Telling me to take the popcorn and jam—Lindsey said it was okay, but it wasn't okay with the boss and it made me look bad. That was small potatoes, because now it's liquor and cigarettes that're missing. There's money in that. I think Lindsey's reselling them, but she told the boss it's me doing it. Plus she's mad because Dave's always flirting with me. Not that I asked him to."

"Dave? Yuck."

Her mom smiled for the first time. "I know. Not my type."

Ivy woke up late that night to hear her mom talking to someone. She tiptoed out of her room and stood in the hall.

"Yeah, you were right about her," her mother said sadly.

There was a pause. Then she said, "I'm sorry too, George. I

just—I have a temper, I always have. It's the way I am, I can't help it."

Another silence.

Her mom laughed softly. "Maybe," she said. "Maybe we could."

Ivy went back to bed and put her pillow over her head.

Ferris Wheel

30

Ivy sat on the floor in front of the computer, her legs numb from sitting cross-legged so long. Her mom sat on the couch behind her, watching *The Price Is Right*. The show's theme song blared.

Ivy fiddled with the fade-in on the shots she'd downloaded, making the transitions slower, then faster, then slower again. The computer Aunt Connie had bought on sale years ago sat on the coffee table between the couch and TV and it was a noisy spot when her mom was home. The movie was more of a movie-ette, really, only a hundred and fifty seconds long, but it was a start. She was getting better with the camera, anyway.

Today's shots were of doors, which Ivy'd always liked. She loved the door to the Everses' house the first time she saw it. It had faded, friendly paint that was the same red as the barn, and a shiny black porcelain knob. It seemed to promise something nice lay within, and it did. Of course, sometimes doors promised one thing and delivered another, but they all seemed to hint at something. That's what she liked about them—the story on the other side.

Ivy pushed a key and the movie began to play. It included a blue door at a bakery across town, Quail Middle School's big glass doors, the small sage-green doors of the old Senate House, and the gate of the wrought-iron fence at the house she liked so much. That one wasn't technically a door, but it was an entrance. Right now the movie ended with their own door and Ivy couldn't decide about that, whether to leave it in or take it out. She tapped a few keys and the their door was gone. She tapped again and it was back.

"You want to watch *Jeopardy!*?" her mom asked.

Ivy shook her head. An ad for the summer carnival down on the river came on and Ivy blocked the sound out. When her mom left the room, Ivy ignored that too. She turned off the computer and opened up her sketchbook. Lately she'd been thinking she could turn the story she'd been working on, about a girl named Heather Lake, into a movie script. It had started out as a story in her sketchbook before she ever left the Everses, and now it was the best idea she had for a movie. In the story, Heather had been kidnapped as a toddler by a woman she thought was her mother.

SCENE ONE she wrote in big block letters at the top of a

new page. SETTING: *A small bedroom with one window, a single bed, and a desk. A cat is curled up on the bed. A girl sits at the desk, reading.*

Ivy gazed at the word *reading,* then erased it. *Writing in a notebook,* she put down instead.

Her mom came back in, dressed in her favorite jeans and her sandals with the high-stacked heels. She held her T-R-A-C-Y key chain in one hand. "Come on. Let's go out."

Ivy looked up. "What?"

"You've been working long enough, you're going to ruin your eyes, to say nothing about your back. How can you sit slouched over like that so long? It can't be good for you."

Ivy sat up straight. Her back did ache.

"We'll go to the carnival. Get something to eat, a corn dog or whatever. Can't sit around the house moping forever."

Ivy scrambled to her feet and yanked her T-shirt straight. The shirt was red with a picture of a laughing atom on it, and it had reminded her of Jacob when she saw it at a garage sale down the street last week. The caption under the picture said *Never trust an atom, they make up everything,* and it had instantly become her official *I'm-working-on-my-movie* shirt, her lucky charm. She always felt good wearing it. Hopeful, and full of possibilities.

In the parking lot at the carnival, Ivy and her mom slammed their doors at the same time. Her mom rapped the roof of the

Mustang. "Jinx." Ivy grinned. Her mom threw her arm over Ivy's shoulders as they headed for the park.

The Ferris wheel curved against the sky and tinny oompah music floated toward them.

Her mother paid the entry fee and they put their hands out to be stamped with a purple-ink clown face, and then they were swallowed by the crowd. Ivy smelled candy apples, French fries, caramel corn, and hamburgers. The rides blared music, the games buzzed and honked, the barkers cried out insistently. Her mom walked to the booth where you bought tickets for the rides, then handed Ivy twenty tickets and took twenty for herself.

"Wow, are you sure? I don't need so many—"

"Don't worry about it, it's a splurge. You only live once, right?"

"Yeah, but, Mom—" Ivy didn't want to finish the sentence—*you haven't been working.*

"No worries." Her mom smiled crookedly. "It's twenty bucks, it won't make or break us. I never did take you out for your birthday, so consider it a belated present."

"Wow. Okay."

"What do you want to ride first? What about the Gravitron? You up for it?"

"Yeah." Ivy buttoned her tickets into the pocket of her shorts and hurried after her mother.

• • •

An hour later they sat side by side in the Ferris wheel. The wheel had stopped when they were almost to the top, and their seat swung slightly. Ivy gripped the safety bar and gazed out over the river. It was almost dark. Below them the festival galloped on. A fierce, sailing joy filled her chest. Her mom touched her knee. "Your dad and I used to always go to all the fairs around. Play the games, ride the rides." She grimaced. "Back in the day. It was a good time."

Ivy's mom never talked about her dad. She probably wished she hadn't said anything now, because her leg started jiggling, which made their seat swing. Ivy studied the lights of the town across the river, pretending that nothing strange had just happened, but she snuck a look at her mom when the wheel started slowly moving again. Her mom tapped her unlit cigarette on the safety bar. "I'm doing pretty good with this quitting thing, hey? Almost two weeks without falling off the wagon. Who'd of thought I'd quit before Walt Evers?"

Ivy frowned. Dad Evers's name was Walton, not Walt, but her mom never would remember that. The wheel began clanking around again. When their car reached the bottom, the man running the ride reached to unhook their bar and Ivy leaned forward to leave, but her mom put her hand out with more tickets.

"What do you say we go around again?" she asked the carnival worker.

"You gotta get out, get back in line." His voice was bored.

Ivy's mom tapped his wrist with the tickets and gave him a playful smile. "C'mon. Give a girl a break."

He shrugged and took the tickets and pulled the lever to make their car move on. "*Step* right up," he yelled to the next people in line. "*Ride* the Ferris wheel, *see* the city from on high."

"So I'm going to give George another shot after all," her mom said as the wheel began to turn. "We're going to try dating again, see how it goes."

Ivy frowned. "You are? Why?"

Her mom shrugged. "I don't know—I guess I just don't like being single."

Ivy stared at the crowd below.

When the wheel stopped again with them at the top, her mom spread her hands flat on the bar and studied them like she was looking for chips in her nail polish.

"Listen, Ives. There's something else I want to say to you."

"Oh?" Ivy's foot began to jiggle nervously. She made it go still. "What?"

"You work so hard, Ives. At school and all. It's kind of amazing. I never was any good at school, I wouldn't have thought you'd be either."

"Well, but I like school. I want to, maybe, go to college."

"College?" Her mom laughed.

Ivy wove her fingers together and tried to feel each one individually: these were her fingers, each one was distinct.

"I mean, it's good I guess. It's not *bad*. But you work too hard, Ives. You try too hard. I don't think that part of it's a good thing. Not for you."

The last of the happiness Ivy had felt since they pulled up at the carnival leaked away. The hole she so often felt inside herself was really there.

"I see how much you want to win this contest thing. And I admire your grit, Ives, I do. But you're putting too much into it. You know you can't win. Right? Don't you?"

Ivy opened her mouth. Nothing came out.

Her mother tapped the bar. "Hon. You've got to remember who you are."

The blood drained from Ivy's head; her feet felt cast in concrete. It was amazing she didn't tip the Ferris wheel over, she was so heavy. She said, slowly, "Who is that, Mom? Who am I?"

Her mom leaned close and looked into her eyes. "You're a Blake. And people like us don't get happy endings. That's why I'm giving George another go."

"Oh? What do you mean?" Ivy's voice sounded flatter than one of Mom Evers's pancakes. She felt the weight of an entire ocean pressing down on her.

"Yeah. Because, you know, he's better than nothing. Better than being alone."

Ivy's heart swam in her chest, a sad fish in a lonely fishbowl. She gazed out at the carnival without seeing anything. *You're not alone,* she wanted to say. *I'm right here. I'm not nothing.* She didn't say anything at all for the whole rest of the evening. Her mom didn't seem to notice.

The Heron

31

"Ivy! You ready?"

Ivy grabbed her bag off her bed and headed for the living room. Her mom had the car keys in her hand and was sliding her feet into her sandals.

"Do I have to come with you today?"

"Yes."

"Why?"

"Because I said so, that's why."

"It's not fair. You and George never pay any attention to me. Now that you're all happily reunited. *Dating* and everything."

Her mom slung her purse over her shoulder. "You're fine, you've got your camera. Work on your movie or whatever."

Ivy plodded after her to the car. "How am I supposed to do

that? There's not even a computer. You have to edit stuff, you know."

"You'll figure it out." Her mom backed onto the street and Ivy stared out the window.

"How's the movie coming, anyway?"

Ivy flicked a disbelieving look at her.

"You're still working on it, right?"

"Like you care. You don't even think I should do it."

"Just because I tried to make you see reality doesn't mean I don't care."

Ivy rolled her eyes at herself in the car window.

"What's it about, anyway?"

"I dunno," Ivy mumbled.

Her mom flipped on her blinker and turned onto the high-way. "Fine, don't tell me." She switched on the radio.

But Ivy had been telling the truth. She was still determined to enter the contest, mostly because she'd told herself she would, but she hadn't known how hard it was going to be to make a movie. Every time she decided to stop, however, she heard Ms. Mackenzie in her head, saying, *Amaze yourself,* and *Promise,* and *Whatever you do, don't quit.*

"I'm going to take a walk, okay?" she asked her mom as soon as they got to George's. George and her mom were smashed together on the couch, making goo-goo faces at each other.

"A walk where?"

"To the river—to the Walkway."

"What for?"

Ivy silently held up her camera.

"Fine. Be careful, don't talk to strangers."

"I won't," Ivy said, but George was tickling her mom and her mom didn't hear her.

The river was just over a mile away. When she got there, Ivy pulled out her camera and headed for the Walkway, the old railroad bridge that had been turned into a footpath. A man on a unicycle was wheeling past the gates. His back was straight, his face serene; his feet made steady circles with the pedals. Ivy felt too shy to film him. She pointed her camera at the water and walked slowly forward.

The closest people were a young couple dressed in blue shorts and white T-shirts a hundred feet ahead. Ivy sighed, annoyed with herself for missing out on the unicycling man. Film with no one in it wouldn't be very interesting. Just as she was thinking that, someone walked into her frame. Ivy saw blue plaid sneakers. Then she was looking through the viewfinder at Grammy Evers.

Grammy's expression swam from surprise to delight. "Ivy Blake, as I live and breathe!" Her voice was so loud that the matching-outfits couple turned to look.

Ivy lowered the camera. "Hi, Grammy. Wow, it's weird to run into you in Poughkeepsie. You're back from your trip, then."

"Two weeks, almost."

Ivy nodded, tapping her finger nervously on the camera's Record button. She knew exactly how long the trip had been over.

"Well, don't just stand there, child. Get over here and give me a hug."

Ivy hesitated, then stepped into Grammy's arms. "So how was the trip?" she asked when she'd stepped away again. "Did you have a good time?"

"Splendid. The weather was perfect, Tecumseh's vegetable garden was thriving, the blackberries were starting to ripen in the woods—it looks like it'll be a bumper crop this year—and Dorothy Peacock got us tickets to a music show in Asheville. Even Tecumseh came down off his mountain to see it."

"Wow." Ivy gazed at the hills and trees across the shore.

"He ended up having the best time of anyone, wouldn't you know? He was clapping and singing along and making a regular fool of himself. Dorothy and Prairie and I were so beat we could hardly keep our eyes open, but he just couldn't leave until the very last minute."

"That sounds fun." Ivy stared at her boots. She pictured herself using them to stamp out the wildfire of jealousy that had sprung up inside her.

"He was so wound up we had to go out to the Big Boy for hot fudge ice cream cakes and coffee, after. He only could be persuaded to head home at midnight and it was nigh onto one before we got there. Cranky as a wet hen the next day."

"Funny." Ivy tapped the Record button again.

"What about you? I see you got your camera."

"Yes."

"You're working on your movie, then? You're going to enter it in that contest?"

"I know I won't win, but—" Ivy lifted a shoulder.

"Why would you say that? You don't know any such thing."

Ivy shrugged again. "It's just obvious."

Grammy frowned. Then she said, "How's your mother?"

"Oh, you know. The same."

Grammy smooched her lips out. Her face looked more like an old wrinkled apple than ever. "And what exactly does that mean?"

"Well, I guess if you ask her, she's never been better."

Grammy snorted.

"She and George got back together."

"How nice."

Grammy didn't bother to sound sincere, which Ivy appreciated. "And she got fired from her job—"

"Uh-oh."

"Yeah. But anyway, she called him up after she got fired, to have somebody to talk to, I guess, and they've been back together ever since."

Grammy laid her arm across Ivy's shoulders and they looked out at the water together. "I do love to watch a river move. It's like life. Ebbs and flows."

Something knotted up inside Ivy loosened, just a little.

"'Men may come and men may go, but I go on forever,'" Grammy said in a quoting voice. "Alfred, Lord Tennyson. 'The Brook.'"

Ivy sighed softly.

"You too, I'll bet. Love the water, I mean. Love to be near it, love to watch it."

Ivy nodded.

Grammy squeezed Ivy's shoulder. "My Knasgowa."

Tears pricked Ivy's eyes. Grammy started to say something more when a woman walked up to them carrying a bakery bag. "Sorry it took so long for me to get back. You should've come with me."

Grammy raised her brows. "It takes what it takes, and you're quite capable without me. What kind did you get?"

The woman rolled her eyes. "Apricot blintzes," she said, speaking deliberately. "Raspberry rugelach. And something called a knish."

"Oh, those are good."

"Is it *nish* or *k-nish*? I didn't know."

"I don't know either," Grammy said cheerfully. The woman made a face. Grammy grinned at her. "Leola, I want you to meet a friend of mine, Ivy Blake. Ivy's pretty much a member of our family, Lord help her."

Leola nodded. She was thin, with grayish-blond hair held back in a ponytail. If Ivy'd been casting her in a movie, she'd have been a house cleaner, or maybe someone who took tolls on the highway. "Nice to meet 'cha," she said.

"Nice to meet you too."

"Leola and I've been doing some work together at the library," Grammy said.

Ivy nodded. Maybe this was the lady Grammy'd been helping to learn how to read when she volunteered at the library. Something studious about the way Leola had asked about *nish* or *k-nish* and frowned at Grammy's answer made her think so.

A few awkward seconds passed. Then Ivy smiled politely; her throat felt tight and sore. "Well, it's nice to meet you, Leola," she said. "It's good to see you, Grammy. I have to get going now. I have to do some camera work. Tell Prairie I said hi, okay? And Mom and Dad Evers. Tell Mom Evers I hope she's feeling okay."

Grammy seemed about to say something, but Leola shifted on her feet and switched the bakery bag to her other hand. Grammy nodded, looking doubtful. "All right, then. Make sure you call. I know you're busy, but you come and see us, all right?"

"Sure," Ivy said. She would. When she had her life as well balanced as the man on the unicycle.

32

Tea

The phone rang at nine a.m. a few days later. "Ivy!" Ivy's mom yelled from the kitchen. "Phone!"

Ivy jogged from her room. Maybe Prairie was calling. The thought that she should've called Prairie first popped up in her head. She squished it down again. "Hello?" she said eagerly.

"Hi. Ivy? This is you, right?"

Ivy frowned. "Yeah—"

"It's Tate! I just got your message from the other day. Me and my mom went to visit my aunt in Pittsburgh. Bo-ring! Anyway, what're you doing?"

"Oh. I'm—nothing, really. What are you?"

"*Nothing.* I'm totally tired of practicing piano. It's too nice out to be inside. Do you want to do something? Maybe go to the pool after lunch? I go to the one down by the river usually."

Ivy stared at the washer churning away. She glanced at her mom, who was drinking coffee. The only reason she'd be up this early was if they were going to George's again. "Um, sure. I'll ask if I can. If my mom says yes, I'll meet you there."

Ivy held the receiver against her stomach and asked if she could go swimming with Tate.

"Who's Tate?"

"She was in my class, she's nice, she's good at math, she wants to go swimming. Can I? She's the only friend I even sort of made here."

"What pool?"

"The one down by the river."

Her mom stared into her coffee cup. Then she said, "Okay, fine."

Ivy pushed through the door of the pool's snack bar half an hour before Tate was supposed to show up. A big bank of clouds had blown in and a drizzling rain started falling. She paid for a cup of tea and slid into a table by the windows and dragged her sketchbook out.

At the table next to her, a couple sat with a baby and a little girl. The mom wore a tie-dyed dress and carried the baby in a sling. The dad had round wire-rimmed eyeglasses and a cap made of patchwork pieces. The girl was in a white dress with pink polka dots. She held three tea bags in one hand and studied them gravely. "Which one do I want, Mom?"

The mom—who'd been gazing down at the baby—tilted her head. "You can pick, whichever one. Probably one with no caffeine in it."

"This one?" The girl held up a tea bag in a blue foil wrapper.

"What's it say on it?"

"Purse—Purrzz—Per Simon."

"Persimmon. Yeah, you'd like it, I think."

"Persimmon. Okay."

"Tear it open at the corner," the dad said. "See the notch? Tear there."

The girl tore the packet open and dropped the bag in her cup.

"Then you pour the hot water over—Dad'll do that—and leave it in there for a while. You steep it. That's what gives it flavor."

"*Steep*? Like a staircase?"

The mom shifted the baby, who stayed curled up, sleeping. "Yeah, good question. *Steep* as in—I don't know. They must have different roots, *steep* and *steep*. It's just what it's called when you leave the tea in the hot water for a while. It brings the flavor out."

The girl nodded and mashed the tea bag against the side of her cup with a spoon. A minute later the dad said, "You can take it out now."

The girl lifted the string and the dad reached over to help. "I always use a spoon," the mom said, and the dad picked one up.

"I wrap the string around it and squeeze." The dad began to do this, but the girl reached out and he let her take over.

Ivy gazed at them longingly.

"She's five going on fifty," the mother said, catching her eye.

Ivy blushed and bent her head over her sketchbook to work on her script again, but instead she started to draw the family—the mom cradling the baby, the dad smiling at the little girl, who seemed solemn for her age until she laughed. It was a simple scene, but also not, of course. Ivy dropped her head onto one hand and her pencil moved more slowly. When she was this girl's age—

Tears brimmed in her eyes. She erased them with a swift rub of her palm. Everyone's life was different.

She picked up her pencil and wrote SCENE FIVE: *Heather's Discovery.*

"Hey! Ivy!" Tate hurried across the room and slid into the other chair at Ivy's table. "I can't believe it's raining, the one day I want to go swimming. Oh well." She tapped Ivy's sketchbook. "What are you doing?"

"Working on my movie."

Tate scooted her chair around so they were side by side. "What's it about?"

"It's about a girl—" But it was hard to explain. Ivy leafed back to the outline she'd started the night of the carnival and passed it to Tate.

Tate wound a strand of hair around a finger and began to read. She made a small *hmm* noise that sounded interested as her eyes moved down the page, and Ivy leaned forward. "It started out as a story, way last winter. This girl named Heather Lake was kidnapped as a toddler. It was okay in a way—she didn't know she'd been kidnapped—but it was lonely. The lady who took her kept her hidden away. Partly so she wouldn't get caught, and partly to protect her."

"Protect her?"

"Her legs are crippled. The kidnapper's sure she can't do stuff other kids can. That's part of the reason she took her. She saw Heather at a swimming pool with her mom and she was horrified that her mom had her in the water. She was sure it was dangerous, which it really wasn't—"

"It was probably good for her."

"*Right*. But the lady didn't know that. And even though Heather's smart and strong and stuff, she believes what her supposed-mom tells her. She never swims in the pool or even leaves the estate—"

Tate squinted at Ivy. "*Never*? What about school? Does the lady hire a tutor or something?"

"Yeah, a tutor, that's a good idea, I didn't think of that." Ivy wrote down *tutor* and underlined it. "Anyway, Heather believes the stuff the woman tells her, that the water's dangerous, the whole world is. Except then somehow she figures out she's been kidnapped and that she has a long-lost sister. She'll have to go on a journey to find her."

"Interesting." Tate bent to study Ivy's outline again. Ivy watched the tea-drinking family pack up their things and leave. A wave of sadness washed over her. The story was made-up, of course, but Ivy could sympathize with Heather. It was like her mom telling her that they weren't lucky people, that Blakes didn't get happy endings.

Tate tapped the sketchbook. "What if Heather has to cross a big lake to find her sister, since she's so afraid of water? You could make her have to take a canoe or kayak across it. You could get one of those to film. We could rent one from the livery—"

Ivy stared at Tate. "That is a *really* good idea." Meeting Tate here was going to be the best part of her day, even with the sadness that had sloshed over her a minute before.

"So maybe she hires a taxi to get to this lake—"

"No, she takes a bus." Ivy was sure about that. She wrote it down.

"And then when she gets there—"

The phone in Ivy's satchel began its old-fashioned ring and Ivy pulled it out. She didn't recognize the number that came up on the screen.

Frowning, she pushed the Talk button. A police officer introduced himself and Ivy listened.

A moment later she was stuffing her things into her satchel.

"What's wrong? What happened?" Tate handed Ivy a pencil that had rolled onto the floor.

"Something bad. My mom's in trouble. I'm sorry, I have to go. I'll call you pretty soon, okay? I'm really sorry—" Ivy jammed her sketchbook in on top of everything else and ran for the door without even snapping the bag's buckles closed.

Trouble

The police were waiting at the house when Ivy pedaled up, panting.

"We're going to take you down to the station," the officers with the nicest eyes said. "Your mom's there, you can see her."

"But what—"

"Try not to worry. We'll explain more at the station."

Ivy sat in a meeting room with her mother. A woman the officers called Lieutenant sat across the table. She had calm eyes that looked as if they'd seen almost everything. For some reason, that comforted Ivy a little. Also, she'd asked if Ivy wanted anything to drink when she got here and had someone bring a cup of hot tea. Ivy cradled the cup in her hands.

"Ivy, your mom is here because her friend George is in the hospital getting his eye looked at," the lieutenant said. "He might lose his sight in it, or maybe have spots drift across it for the rest of his life. He says your mom hit him with a rolled-up magazine. Hit him hard."

Ivy glanced at her mom. Her mom looked down at her hands, which were clenched in her lap.

"She might have detached his retina. Also, his front window was shattered. He says your mom heaved a boom box through it, and that's a vandalism charge."

Ivy looked at her mom again. Her mom sat stone-faced.

"So the next thing that's going to happen for you is that you'll be taken into protective custody."

"Mom?" Ivy said in a wavery voice.

Her mom flashed her a brief sad glance. "I'm sorry, Ives," she said. She stared down at her hands again.

"Mrs. Marsden from Family Services will be here soon," the lieutenant told Ivy as she led her from the room.

"Okay," Ivy answered in a tiny voice.

Ivy spent the night in a group home and half the next day in the offices of Family Services, either being asked questions or sitting in a hard plastic chair, waiting.

The next morning, Mrs. Marsden drove her to the house where she was going to live, at least for a while.

Ivy gaped as they pulled up to it. It was the house she always stopped to admire on her way to school, the one with the wrought-iron fence and glassed-in porch and turret and banks of flowers.

34

Window Seat

"So, welcome," the lady who owned the house said after Mrs. Marsden left. "I'm Beryl Green, like Mrs. Marsden said. You can call me Beryl."

Ivy nodded.

"So I think maybe you walk this way to school?"

After a moment, Ivy nodded again. Her walks to school from the house on O'Reilly Street already belonged in the distant past, in a different lifetime.

The woman—*Beryl*—quirked her lips. She pointed her crutch—it was short and braced by a cuff on her forearm—down the hall. "I gave you the turret. Thought you might like it, but say if you don't. Say if it freaks you out or something. I've never been a foster parent before—you're my first stab at the job—so I don't exactly know what kids like."

"It will be fine. Thank you." In any other circumstances, it would have been fantastic.

"Go to the end of the hall, the door to the stairs is on the left. There's a light switch. On the right, kind of hard to find. Not where you're looking for it. I don't get up there myself much anymore, not since the accident." Beryl waved a crutch in explanation.

Ivy pasted a sympathetic expression onto her face. "I'm sorry."

"It's ten years ago now, I'm used to it more or less. Got T-boned in an intersection. A guy ran a light and *boom*, instant life changer. In the hospital for months, lost my big job at the investment firm—I do all right working from home now, though—and then the icing on the cake, my fiancé pulled the plug on our wedding."

"That was a mean thing to do," Ivy said softly.

Beryl laughed. "For the best in the long run. Who'd want to marry somebody who'd throw you under the bus like that? I'm better off without him, but yeah, it was no fun at the time. Any-hoo, the doc had to put pins in my hip and both legs, so I don't do stairs so well, but I used to love it up there. A friend of mine made the bed and took up towels. Someone you know, actually. She told me she was your teacher, when she heard who was coming to stay with me."

Ivy's heart lurched. "Ms. Mackenzie?"

"Yep, Geena. My best friend since high school. I was at her

birthday party back in May, and I think—well, I might've already sort of met you then."

Ivy bit her lip. So it must have been Beryl's crutch she stumbled over when she was running out of the Really Fine Diner after her mom threw her sketchbook at the wall.

Beryl grimaced. "Anyway, never mind all that. You should check out your room. Say if there's something you need that you don't see."

Ivy squeezed her suitcase handle. It had been Aunt Connie's. It was brown pleather and gigantic. Big enough to hold pretty much everything Ivy owned.

"You'll have to haul your stuff up yourself. I'm no help, sorry to say."

"That's all right."

"There's a phone in the den." Beryl pointed in the opposite direction with her crutch. "Your friend—Prairie, right? such a cool name—called. She wants you to call her. I guess Mrs. Marsden called her parents because you stayed with them before."

Ivy nodded.

"She said you didn't want to go back to them?"

"They're—really busy this time of year." The fact was, Ivy hadn't wanted them to know. She hadn't wanted to be any more ashamed than she was already, she hadn't wanted them to realize how bad things really were, and most of all she didn't want to bother them. Mom Evers's due date was soon; they didn't need Ivy's problems piled on top of them.

Beryl's green eyes watched her closely. "Well, use the phone whenever you want. And come down to the kitchen when you're done unpacking, I'll get you something to eat. I made salmon for lunch, with wild rice and broccoli. Turned out well, if I do say so."

"Okay. Thank you," Ivy said, even though she didn't intend to use the phone and she wasn't hungry, either. She made herself smile before she trudged off with her suitcase because Beryl seemed nice enough. Different than she'd imagined when she saw her reading on the porch. More abrupt, less dreamy, but still nice. Ivy was lucky, there. As lucky as a Blake could get, anyway.

The room at the top of the turret was octagonal, so the furniture sat at angles. There was an antique bureau, a bed with a blue wool blanket, a braided rug, and a nightstand. The nightstand had claw feet, and for an instant Ivy was pleased about that.

She lifted her suitcase onto the bed and unzipped it. She took her clock from the T-shirt she'd wrapped around it and put it on the nightstand. She unpacked her socks and underwear into the top drawer of the bureau and put her dresses and shirts and shorts in the middle one. She zipped the suitcase back up—all that was left inside was her quilt, which she couldn't bear to have out reminding her of the Everses and happy times—and put it in the closet. Next was the camera. She knelt on the floor and pulled the bottom bureau drawer open and set the Life Savers box with the camera packed into it inside. She gazed down at it. Then she pushed the drawer shut.

She made sure the drawer fronts lined up with the bureau frame exactly, then put her book bag on a peg in the closet. It hung limp, with only a few pencils in it. Her sketchbook was missing again. The only thing Ivy could figure was that it must have dropped out of her bag as she ran from the snack bar at the pool.

She closed the closet door and looked around the room. The blanket was smooth on the bed and the top of the bureau was bare except for some towels. The only sign she was there was her boots. Ivy put them in the closet and closed the door again.

After that there was nothing left to do. She crossed the room and sat in the turret's window seat and looked down at the garden.

35

Love, Ivy

Beryl rustled the newspaper, which got thrown onto the porch every morning at seven. "There's an art class up at the library you could take, if you wanted. Pencil sketching."

Ivy bit into her toast. It was sourdough, from a bakery Beryl liked, the one with the blue door. Ivy steered her thoughts away from her door movie and considered the row of numbers in front of her. If she put a two in the fifth slot down, a three could go in the top left corner.

"Geena told me about your drawing. What do you think? Sound interesting?"

"No. Thank you, though." Ivy bounced her pencil on her Sudoku book. She'd gotten addicted to Sudoku lately.

The old-fashioned clock ticked from its spot on the dining room's credenza and the fan Beryl kept running on the floor whirred. Ivy spooned another blob of strawberry jam onto her toast. Even though it was store-bought, it was nearly as good as what Mom Evers and Grammy made, almost like eating the berries fresh. The tag on the top of the jar said $12.99, which had made Ivy blink when she read it. She tried not to be a pig about it, but Beryl said there was plenty more where that came from, and some mornings Ivy splurged.

Today was so peaceful—it was sunny and the wind chimes that hung on the side porch were tinkling and Beryl's cat, Perkin, was dozing on the rug by the kitchen door—that the old Ivy might've chosen this moment as the best part of her day. For sure she would have been pretending she belonged here in this big old house with its wooden floors and pocket doors and stained glass windows.

The new Ivy did not pretend that. She didn't choose best parts—what was the point?—or pretend anything either. She did treat herself to an extra helping of jam, however. She lifted the toast and the smell of berries filled her nose. She studied the puzzle's rows and columns, double-checking her logic before she wrote the three in. She hated erasures.

"There's a watercolor class too—"

Ivy shook her head and wrote in the three in the top left square. "I don't think so."

"Just thought you might get a kick out of it."

Ivy skipped a glance at her like a stone skipped across water. "Thank you, anyway."

The phone rang and Beryl clumped her leg down from the chair she had it up on and grabbed her crutch.

Ivy put her pencil down. "I can go."

"No, I need to move. Stiffen up if I sit too long."

Ivy nodded. Beryl was firm about being able to do things, almost prickly, and Ivy had learned in the week or so she'd been here not to argue.

In the den, Beryl said, "Patience! Yes, we're fine. Eating breakfast."

A moment passed. Then Beryl exclaimed, "Oh, my! A little boy. Or a big boy, I should say—nine pounds! That's great, I'm so glad everything's all right. Here, hold on, I'll get Ivy—"

Ivy slid off her chair and slipped out the back door.

She headed for the swing that sat under a mammoth pine tree at the farthest edge of the yard, below a little dip the ground made on its way down to the goldfish pond. The seat had a thick layer of pine needles on it when Ivy found it. It'd taken half a day for the wood slats to dry out after she brushed them off.

She swept the needles off every day now. Sometimes she looked at the small quiet pond and the slowly swimming fish, but mostly she did Sudoku. She got two more done while she was there this time.

Beryl was back at the dining room table when Ivy went inside, working at her laptop. She wore half glasses with purple frames, and her eyes darted back and forth as she read. She didn't look up when Ivy came in. Her work was something to do with analyzing stocks and start-up ventures and it sounded complicated. Ivy always tried to be extra quiet when Beryl was busy with it. She slid back into her chair and pressed the Sudoku book open to a new page. The puzzle was labeled *Hard*. She began to examine it.

Beryl took off her glasses. "So, the phone was Mrs. Evers. The elder Mrs. Evers."

Ivy almost said *I know*. "Oh?" She looked Beryl in the eye and made sure not to fidget.

"Imagine my surprise to find you gone when I got in here."

"I went outside."

"So you did," Beryl said. "So you did."

She put her glasses back on and went back to work. After a minute though, she broke her disapproving silence—Ivy knew Beryl was disappointed in her, maybe almost as much as Ivy was disappointed in herself—and said that Mom Evers had the baby at eight thirty-six that morning, a boy they'd named Daniel Walton. He weighed nine pounds, two ounces, and was in perfect health. Also, according to Grammy Evers, he was extremely handsome and obviously highly intelligent. "All of which you could've heard firsthand if you hadn't ducked out."

Ivy rolled her lips in. Beryl frowned with her brows furrowed. Then she heaved a sigh that was like setting a heavy bag down and gave Ivy a rueful smile. "Dealing with life's a real pain sometimes, isn't it?" She pulled her glasses out of her hair and went back to work.

Ivy lingered at the table after dinner. She brushed crumbs off the tablecloth and straightened the candlesticks, which made her think of Mrs. Grizzby. She wondered how her daughter's visit had gone. Maybe Ivy would stop by one of these days. Say hello, drink soda from a tiny jelly glass. See if she could make Mrs. Grizzby flash out that radiant smile that hid inside her.

Beryl was headed for the porch with a book. "What's up?" she asked when she noticed Ivy lingering.

"I wondered if you have some pieces of paper. Blank pieces. And pencils. Colored pencils, maybe?"

Ivy expected Beryl's eyes would light up and she'd start asking questions, but Beryl only said, "Sure. In the den, in the desk, bottom drawer."

Ivy came back with a pad of vellum paper, a metal tin containing thirty-six colored pencils, and an unopened package of sketching pencils with a white gum eraser included.

"Ordered it all online after the accident," Beryl said when Ivy held the things up questioningly. "Had an idea I'd entertain myself while I recuperated, get creative, tap into the other side of my brain. Never did get around to it."

"I never saw paper this expensive before."

"Use it. I'm never going to."

"I don't want to waste it." The price tag was still on it: $39.99 for fifty pieces.

"Just sitting there, that's what I call wasted. Make paper airplanes out of it if you feel like it. Anything'd be better than its current use. Non-use, that is."

Ivy sat down and gently opened the pad of paper. She gingerly pried the lid off the tin box to reveal the pencils. She held up the package of sketching pencils. "These too? It's okay? To open them?"

"I said so, didn't I?"

Ivy opened the bag and slid the contents out onto the table and gazed at them with a feeling of quiet joy.

"I know what it's like, you know."

Ivy's hand stalled above the 6B.

"Getting stopped, sidelined. Derailed, however you want to put it."

Ivy nodded.

"You ever want to talk about it, you can."

Ivy curled her toes inside her boots, which she'd put on before supper. It had seemed like she needed the company. "Okay." She didn't look at Beryl.

"*Do* you want to talk about it?"

"Not right now," Ivy said softly.

Beryl picked up her book from the table where she'd set it. "Fair enough. Just remember, the offer stands."

Three hours later, Ivy leaned back in her chair and stretched her arms out.

She'd drawn the Everses in their kitchen. She'd made Daniel the size of a bag of flour, the closest thing to nine pounds she could think of. He was wrapped in a blue blanket in Mom Evers's arms, and Mom Evers was smiling down at him. She looked beautiful, even though Ivy'd had to make her hair fall over most of her face to cover up how wrong her nose had come out. Prairie was grinning, dressed in her boots and jeans. Her shoulders were crooked and her chin was wrong, but it was obvious who it was meant to be. Ivy was proudest of Dad Evers. He looked almost exactly like himself: lanky and shy, with black hair that parted itself on one side. Grammy stirred sugar into a dimpled blue cup and Pup sat near the woodstove, licking his paw.

Ivy added one last hint of shading to the stove, then opened the card up and gazed at the blank inside.

After a minute she wrote *Congratulations!*

She tried to think of what else to say. In the end she just wrote *Love, Ivy.*

The Family Silver

"Muhammad won't come to the mountain, the mountain will come to Muhammad."

Grammy stood on Beryl's porch cradling a white bakery box and gripping a photo album against her side with one elbow. A brightly striped gift bag with pink rope handles dangled from three fingers of one hand.

Ivy gaped at her. The doorbell had gonged and she'd raced down from upstairs because she knew Beryl was just getting out of the shower.

"I was thinking you'd invite me in."

"I—wow. *Grammy.* Yes, come in! I thought you'd be the FedEx guy for Beryl."

"Nope."

Ivy took the bakery box from Grammy's arms and led her into the front hall.

"Who is it?" Beryl called from the bathroom.

"It's Grammy!"

"Excellent," Beryl hollered. "I'll put coffee on in a minute—Patience, you like coffee?"

"Love it," Grammy hollered back. "I've brought cake."

"Perfect. Go on into the dining room, you two. Ivy, get the good china out of the credenza, and the silver."

A minute later Ivy and Grammy were seated across from each other at the dining room table. Ivy watched Perkin pad toward a patch of sunlight. She was glad Grammy had come but she didn't know what to say. Perkin sat down and began cleaning his paw.

"That was a beautiful card you made," Grammy said.

Ivy rubbed her thumb over a faint scar in the tabletop.

"Loren's got Walton making a frame for it. Looks like you took a long time on it."

"A few hours," Ivy said softly.

"It's clear you meant what you said."

Ivy rubbed harder at the table's shallow scar.

"'Love, Ivy,'" Grammy quoted. "Clear you meant it. Even though we haven't heard much from your corner lately. Clear to me, anyway. And to Walton and Loren."

Ivy exhaled a breath she didn't know she'd been holding,

but she had, for a long time. For weeks. Months, really. Ever since her mother brought her to Kingston in April. Ever since she chose her mom over her friendship with Prairie and then wasn't sure where to put her foot next.

"I wouldn't be surprised if even Daniel gets it, he's such a wonder. I never saw such a bright boy, not since Walton was born. I've brought pictures—"

Grammy patted the photo album and Ivy nodded.

"Prairie's a different story. She's got a bit of a bee in her bonnet. You've hurt her feelings, kiddo."

Ivy ducked her head. Prairie had hurt her feelings too, but Ivy knew she might've been the one to start it, and for sure she hadn't been the one to end it.

"As far as I can tell, it's nonsense, on both your parts. Life is short, forgive fast. Mark Twain said something to that effect."

Ivy studied her feet. They were bare, which seemed wrong, considering the fancy china and silver. She was about to tell Grammy she and Mark Twain were right when Beryl came in.

"Coffee's ready."

Grammy clapped. "Let's haul out that cake. I bought it from a place in New Paltz. Leola—the woman I was with on the Walkway, Ivy—does all their fancy decorating, has for years. And let's get these presents opened too, Knasgowa."

Ivy didn't mean to smile—she didn't much these days—but she couldn't help herself, a grin stole out. There were presents; they were for her.

"So—David's a real wonder, huh?" she said as she reached for a package.

"These are so pretty." Ivy held a teacup up to the light over the sink. Grammy had gone home hours ago and now dinner was over too. She turned the cup. It was so thin she could see her thumb on the opposite side. "I'm scared I'll break them."

"You won't break anything. Besides, they're just things."

"Yeah, but *nice* things. You don't want to go crashing them around."

Beryl stood with her bad hip leaned against the counter, drying plates. She wiped each one tenderly, like a baby's face. "Belonged to my great-great-aunt. The set's been in the family since Lincoln was president."

Ivy held up a fork. "These too?"

Beryl examined the handle. "*These* were from my dad's side. Great-Grandma Myrtle's wedding silver. Didn't seem right to send it to Goodwill, even though I had two sets already. These are the nicest, I think. I like that flare in the handle." Beryl rubbed the fork with her thumb.

"My aunt Connie had silver. Real silver, like this."

"Nice. Was it hers, or your grandmother's, or somebody else's?"

Beryl looked at Ivy expectantly, but now, even though Ivy had been the one to bring the subject up, she didn't want to talk about it. Thinking about the past was too hard. It was like taking the lid off a basket of snakes. Beautiful snakes, like the copperhead she'd watched on TV, but dangerous. There were good memories mixed up with the bad ones and it all made Ivy's throat go tight. "I don't know. I don't remember," she said. She picked up the pan Beryl had used to cook chicken for their supper. "Do I put this in the water, or just wipe it off?"

37

Three A.M.

Ivy woke out of a dream in the middle of the night. She didn't know if it'd been good or bad, only that it left her alert. She looked at her clock. Three a.m.

She wondered what her mother was doing. She imagined her in the orange jumpsuit she'd been wearing when Ivy saw her last week. Mrs. Marsden had picked her up and taken her to the jail. They went through security and a guard led them to a visiting room. Mrs. Marsden patted Ivy's shoulder when her mom came out, then went and sat by the door. Ivy and her mom perched across from each other in low padded chairs that were built to look comfortable, but weren't.

I thought you'd go back with the Everses, her mom had said.

Ivy didn't feel like explaining about that. *They put me with Beryl.*

You like her? This Beryl?

Yes.

Heavy doors clanged; the guards stood watchful. There was a chemical smell. Some cleanser, probably. Her mom sat quietly, looking at Ivy.

The food's not too bad, she said after a while.

That's good.

Finally really quitting the cigarettes. Don't have a choice, you can't have 'em in here.

That's good. That you're quitting, I mean.

It's hard to sleep at night. Noisy. I could do with a shot of something, but of course you can't have that either. Ha.

I'm sorry.

Her mom shook her head. *I don't sleep at night anyway.*

She'd smiled sadly, and then it was time to go.

It was strange, how her mom was in jail—for now, anyway—for hitting George, but had ended up coming home not all that long after shooting Ivy's father. The two things were so different. Except that they both happened in the same kind of moment—one of her mom's crazy angry moments.

Ivy imagined her mom sitting on the edge of a bunk, her head hanging down, her hands clasped together. She imagined her jiggling her leg and wishing for a cigarette. She imagined her getting into an argument. That's what she did when she was mad, or scared, or bored, and it'd be boring in there, especially for her mom, who didn't have hobbies like drawing or reading or weight lifting. Only now—how did Ivy know?—maybe she did.

Ivy reached out a finger to touch the clock's greenly glowing face. She breathed in and out slowly. She told herself to think happy thoughts, or better yet, not to think at all.

Her mind refused to obey. It kept generating pictures: her mom picking up the gun; her mom holding baby Ivy nestled close, like Mom Evers held Daniel in the pictures Grammy had brought. Her mom looking at her pleadingly; her mom throwing her notebook across the diner. Her mom reaching into a popcorn bag and her mom plowing down George's garbage cans. Her mom sitting on the edge of a bunk, lonely and frightened . . .

After an hour Ivy threw the sheet off and poked her feet into the slippers Beryl had given her. The mailman had brought them a few days ago. She shuffled across the room and down the stairs to the kitchen. She would fix herself a cup of tea. Beryl always said to make herself at home. For once, Ivy would.

38

Knasgowa

Ivy filled the kettle and set it on the burner—its flames were like a ring of tiny campfires—and reached for a mug. Her hand brushed against something. She made a little leap and then there was a crash. Perkin yowled and Beryl's light came on in her room down the hall.

"I broke something," Ivy said as soon as Beryl appeared in the kitchen. "I'm sorry. I'll get it fixed—" She looked at the shattered pieces and realized how dumb that sounded. "I mean, I'll buy you a new one."

Beryl limped over and poked at the pieces with the tip of her crutch. "Thank God."

"What?"

"Free at last. Geena gave it to me. Housewarming present. I'm sure it was expensive, it was from that gallery down on the water where they get a king's ransom for everything, but it was hideous. Couldn't say that, of course."

Ivy stood very still. She didn't know whether to believe Beryl or not.

"The thing was a terror. Not my style at all, or hers either I'd have thought, but everybody makes a bad choice sometimes. Listen, get the kettle. The whistling's making me nervous."

Ivy switched the burner off.

Beryl poked again at the broken pieces of teapot. "Probably better sweep it up before we step on it."

Ivy hurried to get the broom and dustpan. When she'd finished, she didn't know what to do next. "I guess I'll go back to bed."

"Don't you want your tea?"

Ivy glanced at Beryl uncertainly. "Do you want some?"

"No, but I'll sit with you, if you want. Maybe you'll tell me what that word meant."

"What word?"

"That name Patience called you. Kennis-something."

"Knasgowa." Ivy smiled. "It's a nickname."

"I figured *that*. But what does it mean?"

"Heron," Ivy said. "It means heron, in Cherokee."

Beryl waited, but Ivy didn't know what else to say. *Knasgowa* was a compliment. Herons were determined and curious. They were good hunters, good at waiting. They were known for being independent. Loners, really. If they were people, they wouldn't like anyone looking over their shoulder, telling them what to do. Sometimes that got them into trouble. Sometimes their eyes were bigger than their stomachs and they tried to bite off—or snatch up, in the case of a fish—more than they could chew. Still, they usually coped. They were survivors.

Ivy had looked it up on the computer at school when Grammy first said it, but she hadn't had to look it up to know what Grammy meant. Being called Heron was a big deal. Also a private deal.

"Like pulling teeth," Beryl said equably when Ivy stayed quiet. "Come on, let's sit in the dining room, my leg's killing me."

The clock on the credenza chimed once: three thirty. Ivy fiddled with the cake server, which Beryl had told her to leave out so she could polish it later. Ivy used to help Aunt Connie polish the silver after holiday dinners. Those were times—getting the silver out, setting the table, smelling the big chicken cooking—when Ivy had felt like a normal kid.

She smiled sadly. Aunt Connie. She told Ivy every drawing she did was *wonderful*, her best yet. She clapped loudly at Ivy's school programs and always did a wolf whistle that was embarrassing. Once Ivy was a tree in a forest of trees in a play, and Aunt Connie insisted she was the best of the bunch, even though she didn't have a single line to speak. *Trees are good,* she'd told Ivy. *They don't have to talk. They just stand tall and strong.*

No matter how bad things were, she had always stayed cheerful, or at least cheerful-ish. *Oh well*, she'd say, looking over whatever the problem was. *Shee-ite happens.* She actually did say that, *shee-ite*, instead of the real word.

It was strange, how two sisters could be so different.

She and Ivy's mom hadn't had a spectacular childhood. She'd told Ivy that, right at the end. *Not to excuse anything*, she said. *Just to, kind of, explain your mama to you. I'll tell you more about it one day.* She'd run out of time, though. It was a talk Ivy guessed neither one of them had much wanted to have.

The clock ticked and Perkin batted at a tinfoil ball. Otherwise the house was silent. Beryl sat with her leg up, her head tipped back, and her eyes shut. Ivy drew a fork toward her, then a spoon, and then the cake knife. "I could polish these," she said. "If you wanted. I used to like polishing my aunt Connie's silver."

She ended up talking more than she meant to. Maybe because it was the middle of the night. Everything was strange; the rules were broken.

"I think about my aunt Connie's stuff a lot." Ivy had never said this to anyone before. She'd never even told Prairie how much time she spent walking through Aunt Connie's house in her head on nights she couldn't sleep. "I miss the weirdest things. Like her blender. Who misses a blender? But she used to make me milk shakes in it. Strawberry banana, chocolate chip coconut, whatever I wanted. And the silver—we used it for every single holiday. Mardi Gras, Earth Day, Halloween, *everything*. She said life was hard enough already without missing the chance to make a party of things—"

Beryl pumped her fist in the air without lifting her head from the back of her chair or opening her eyes. "Agreed. Bravo, Aunt Connie."

Ivy glanced at her; the surface of her skin tingled with a feeling she couldn't pin down. Hope? Love? Or maybe it was trust. "And the Christmas decorations—I really miss those. She had this inflatable Santa sleigh and reindeer she put out on the lawn every winter. It was kind of dumb, but—you know. It was *ours*, it was us."

"Of course it was."

"I miss her collections. She collected *every*thing. Umbrellas, coffee mugs, old postcards, anything to do with a dragonfly—"

Beryl's eyes were still closed but her voice sounded interested. "What happened to all of it?"

"Mom put it in storage." Everything Ivy hadn't grabbed and hidden in her closet.

"Storage. As in—a storage facility?"

"Yes. We jammed everything in. Boxes and boxes. It took forever." Ivy remembered the sound of her mom slamming the storage room door shut. It was like she was shutting the door on that whole part of their life. Ivy hadn't cried at the funeral but she did cry then. Cried and cried, and her mom snapped at her to stop it.

Beryl sat up. "Where is this storage facility?"

Ivy picked up a knife. "In New Paltz."

"You never went back to get the stuff?"

"The house Mom rented was small. Too small to hold it all, I guess." Or maybe it was that her mom had not liked to be reminded of Aunt Connie after she was gone. She never talked about her; she'd get mad if Ivy tried. "Anyway, no, we didn't go back, and then I moved in with the Everses. Mom came to get me in April, and we just never—it's still there, I guess."

"Do you know where the key is?"

Ivy nodded. Her mom had kept the key in her underwear drawer. Ivy had gone into her mom's room to get it while Mrs. Marsden was waiting for her to pack her things. No way was she leaving it in a house she didn't know if she'd ever see again.

"Let's go check it out." Beryl reached for her crutch.

"Now?"

"No time like the present." Beryl thumped her leg to the floor.

"But how would we get there?" Beryl could drive, but she didn't like to, especially not at night.

"I'll call Geena. She's got that big old truck, might as well put it to use."

"But—Beryl—" Ivy looked at the clock on the credenza. She couldn't believe how long they'd sat talking. "It's almost five *a.m.*"

"I know, but trust me, she'll love it. It's exactly the kind of stunt we used to get up to in high school. Plus—well—it's time you caught a break, I think." Beryl clomped to the den and picked up the phone.

The Indy 500

Ivy lay on the Oriental rug in the parlor, one of the forks from Aunt Connie's silver set resting on her chest. A half-finished crocheted blanket in clashing colors lay on the floor beside her. Her mother had been making it, in the time Before—before that terrible night when she picked up the gun.

Ivy had forgotten about it until she opened the box. Then the memory flew into her head: her mom on the couch in front of the TV, her head bent over the blanket. Frowning, yanking at the yarn. There was no great meaning to it. The blanket was just a thing her mom had been doing, a project. Then her mom catapulted them into the time After, and as far as Ivy could think, she'd never undertaken a project again.

Also on the floor was a spray of snapshots, Aunt Connie's silverware box, three model cars (a Thunderbird, a Mustang, and a Camaro), and one ticket to the Indy 500. Ivy picked up the Thunderbird and dangled it over her head. An image of her dad bent over a car with a paintbrush in his hand had raced back when she opened this box. The image of him hunched at the table beneath the shaded lamp that had hung from the ceiling made her throat tighten. He'd been good at painting. The stripes along the Thunderbird's sides were narrow and sure. There wasn't a single drop of paint anywhere it wasn't supposed to be.

The race ticket brought memories back too. She was five. Her favorite cereal back then was Cheerios, her favorite shirt was her blue-and-white-striped one. She heard her mom's voice in her head. Yelling.

We can't afford that!

What, like we can afford those clothes you bought? her dad had said.

I can get myself something decent to wear if I want—

And I can go to a race with some buddies.

You know I hate being alone—

It's one weekend. And you won't be alone, you'll have Ivy—

You and your buddies. When's the last time we did something fun?

Ivy didn't remember what else they said, or if those were the exact words, but that was the idea. She'd blocked it out all these years. It was so ordinary. Nothing to shoot someone over.

She rolled onto her stomach and put her fingertips on the book Grammy'd given her the day she came with the cake. It was *The Invention of Hugo Cabret*, which the movie *Hugo* was based on. She touched the magnet from Grammy next. *Never, never, never give up* it said. Ivy closed her hand around it tight. She had things to consider besides her parents' last fight, things about *now*, things about her. At the moment, she was thinking. She'd been thinking, ever since they got back from the storage facility two days ago.

The doorbell pealed. FedEx, probably. Beryl always had a package to send out for her work, or one coming in. She liked to sign for them herself usually. She was likely to snap if Ivy tried to beat her to the door. "I'm not *crippled*," she'd say. Then, "Well, I am, but I'm not unable."

The doorbell rang again, two gongs in quick succession. "Ivy!" Beryl yelled from the den. "Get that, would you? I'm in the middle of a meeting."

Ivy scrambled to her feet and padded down the hall, the fork in her hand.

Jacob stood on the porch. Ivy gaped at him in astonishment. His T-shirt was green, with a hedgehog on it. *Hedgehogs: Why can't they just share?* it said. He pushed a lock of hair back. "Movie Girl. Finally." He held a paper bag out toward her.

The instant her fingers made contact, Ivy knew what it was. She knew the weight in her hand, the feel of the wire spiral through the bag, the precise hardness of the covers.

"You are not the easiest person to find," he said.

"Where did you—"

"Outside the snack bar at the pool. I thought maybe you saw me—"

Ivy shook her head.

"I work there for the summer. I was emptying the garbage cans when I saw this fly out of your bag."

Ivy's back tensed, remembering the phone call, and the reason for it.

"I thought it was you, but you took off so fast—"

Ivy had never put her name in the journal, not even after Ms. Mackenzie gave it back. It had seemed both unnecessary—it was a part of her, like her fingers—and much too dangerous. Someone might *identify* her with it. "How—"

"I studied the pictures."

Ivy opened the book. There was her life. Captured, restored. She put a finger on the bunch of parsley in the bag of groceries in the back of the station wagon. There was her sneaker, there was Prairie's. She'd forgotten a second small sketch on the same page. The back end of the car with its license plate and the stickers that said *Love your mother, recycle* and *Hunt for Sasquatch!*

She turned to a page further in. There was Ms. Mackenzie at the blackboard. She was pretty recognizable, especially if you'd run into her at the Really Fine Diner. Slowly, Ivy nodded.

He'd tracked down Ms. Mackenzie, then. The two of them had talked about her. But—that was okay.

She looked up at Jacob and confessed abruptly, "I took down one of those posters you put up that day I saw you at the college."

He raised an eyebrow. "Yeah? I designed it, but I didn't think it was *that* good. Not framable or anything. Although you never know—"

"It's okay—"

"Just *okay*?"

Ivy squinted at him, working to hide a grin. "Yeah, it's kind of plain actually—"

He flung a hand to his heart like she'd wounded him. "I was in a hurry! My grandmother asked me to do it, like, one night before she needed it—"

Ivy smiled. "I took it because I want to make a movie. I *am* making a movie. Trying, anyway. To enter in the contest."

Jacob whistled. "Cool."

"Your poster inspired me."

"*Very* cool."

Ivy smiled at the parquet floor.

Jacob crossed his arms and leaned himself on one hip, like he was settling in for a chat and could make himself comfortable anywhere, even standing on a stranger's porch. "I grew up in the movie business. Well, the theater business, anyway.

My grandparents own the old theater in Rosendale, the brick one—"

Ivy's eyes snapped to his. "I love that place!"

He grinned. "Um, yeah." He said it the same way you'd say *duh*. "I've never tried to make a movie, though. That's a radical undertaking. What's yours going to be about?"

Ivy opened the door wider. "That's kind of a long story. Do you want to come in?"

They sat cross-legged on the Oriental rug in the parlor for so long that Ivy's legs went numb. They'd been talking and talking. About Ivy's movie, and about movies in general. Their words had slowed down in the last few minutes, but the quiet felt as natural as conversation, and seemed to hold as much in it.

"What's this?" Jacob picked up the Thunderbird.

Ivy examined him. Hedgehog shirt, hair hanging past his shoulders in mild curls, hazel eyes, crinkled at the corners. There was an ease about him. Also a gravity. She considered telling him it was nothing. But then she thought of how she'd made friends with Prairie last year, so suddenly and completely. She thought of Ms. Mackenzie leaning toward her when she hardly even knew Ivy, telling her that her drawings were great, that she could do whatever she wanted with her life. She thought of Tate offering her apple in exchange for a mushy banana, of Beryl poking at the broken pieces of teapot with her crutch and then smiling. She reached out and put one finger on the Thunderbird's hood. "It was my dad's. He was working on it just before he died."

Jacob's face went still and grave. "Oh, wow, I'm sorry. What happened?"

Ivy told him.

He told her stuff too. He'd lost his younger brother three years before. Cam. Hit in the head by a stray softball. "It was one of those if-only things. If only we'd gone ten minutes later, hung out ten feet farther down the field, if Cam had just turned his head—"

Ivy nodded. You could drive yourself crazy with if-onlys. A lot of them you couldn't do anything about. They sat in your path like huge boulders or a raging river that wasn't written on your map. You might stare at them for a long time before you searched out a long, hard detour around them. Like Ms. Mackenzie said in school that cranky, rainy day, you had to cope.

But some things—you might almost miss them, you could get so used to thinking every obstacle was a gigantic boulder— you could change, or try to. You could attempt to climb up over the rock or sneak your way across a log that spanned the river, and see how it worked out. It was risky, but maybe worth it. If you opened the door wider, picked up the phone, some-times something wonderful could happen.

40

Riding the Bus

Ivy brought her sketchbook to the dining room table after Jacob left. She looked at the last thing she'd written: *Heather takes a bus—*

In a way, Ivy had been on a bus herself these past few weeks. Riding around the world, trying to get off at the right stops, missing them sometimes.

She pulled the postcards Prairie had sent from North Carolina out of the back of the book. Lined up according to the numbers in the bottom right-hand corners, the message read, *I got so mad. Wish you were here, Love, Prairie.* Which was nice. But Ivy was pretty sure the real message was nicer yet. The card with a 1/6 on it must have gotten hung up in the mail somewhere. Ivy would've bet her video camera that it said *I'm sorry.*

I'm sorry I got so mad.

Suddenly, Ivy wanted to be the first one to say she was sorry. She knew she ought to be.

With a brisk flip, she turned to a new page and wrote TO DO at the top with one of her *Senators* pencils. *Call Tate,* she wrote. *Finish script. Get actors.* There were twenty more things on the list, half a dozen of them involving Jacob, who'd already said he'd help. Last of all, Ivy wrote *Call Prairie.*

She could hear Grammy telling her something quote-y and saying-ish: *There's no time like the present* or *Well begun is half done.* Or most likely, *Life's short, forgive fast.*

She went into the den and shut the door. Sat in Beryl's office chair and experimented with raising and lowering it. Poked the hula girl bobble doll that stood by Beryl's pen cup. The hula girl swayed and her tiny grass skirt swished. *"Un-a-li,"* Ivy whispered. The Cherokee word for friend, the first Cherokee word she and Prairie had learned together. She remembered finding the translation site on the Internet, showing it to Prairie, the two of them whispering and giggling and getting yelled at by the librarian. How had they gone from that, to this? Ivy lifted the phone receiver.

"Hi, Prairie?" Her voice wavered. "It's me, Ivy. How are you?"

Prairie said *okay* cautiously and Ivy poked the hula girl again. The doll's painted-on smile seemed sympathetic; she was forever poised to strum a chord on her little ukulele. Ivy sucked in a belly breath, like Ms. Mackenzie had taught them. "I wanted to tell you that I'm sorry I haven't called in so long. And I'm sorry if I acted like a jerk. I was jealous, I guess, about Kelly, and about—well, how nice your family is, when mine's all messy and sad."

"Yeah, but *you're* not messy and sad," Prairie protested. "You're great. You're *you*. And—I don't know—all the messy, sad stuff made you you—" She made that growl of frustration that Ivy'd missed hearing. "This is coming out all wrong, but messy and sad is *not* the main thing about you."

Ivy poked the hula girl again, and the green paper fringes of her skirt swished softly. "Thanks. Anyway, the main thing is, I miss you. I never didn't miss you. I was hoping we could get together pretty soon. Like, really soon. And there's something else. I need help with this movie. A lot of help. I was hoping you'd want to, and maybe Kelly too—"

They said good-bye and Ivy flung herself on the rug. She stretched her muscles and a feeling of contentment, one with fringy edges like the hula girl's skirt, spread out inside her.

41

Red Kayak

Ivy's alarm clock beeped at daylight. She groped for the shut-off button and hoisted herself onto an elbow. Prairie was in the next bed, flat on her back and snoring. Tate was in the bed beyond that, on her side, breathing slow and even. Ivy swung her feet to the floor—pine boards, cool and rough—and pulled her sweater and jeans on and tiptoed to the stairs.

Beryl sat in the kitchen, a half-empty cup of coffee on the table in front of her, her leg propped up on the bench. She had a book open, the pages held flat with the tool for lifting the burners off the cookstove. "You want some eggs?" she whispered.

"I don't think I have time."

"Better make time. I'll fry them, I've got the fire going."

Ivy could feel it. "Well—"

"You need to eat. Going to be a big day."

"Okay."

Beryl slid her leg to the floor. "You want tea?"

"I can make—"

"I'm not *crippled*."

Ivy rolled her eyes. "Actually, you are. But you're not un*able*."

Beryl snorted. "C'mon. Help me figure out where Geena keeps the skillet in this place."

Ten minutes later, Ivy stepped onto the porch of Ms. Mackenzie's cabin with her hands wrapped around a mug of tea. The tea bags were stored in a Folgers can—so the mice wouldn't get at them, Ms. Mackenzie said when she found Ivy and Beryl searching the cupboards—and the can sat on a plank above the stove along with a kerosene lamp, a box of matches, and two dusty candles. The tea was almost boiling. The water'd been heated in a blue speckled pot, the kind you imagined cowboys using over a campfire. It tasted amazing.

Ivy strode off the porch and across the yard and down four mossy, slippery steps made of logs, to the beach. Her breath puffed out into the cool August morning. Mist rose over the water and a jay called from the tiny island that lay a hundred yards offshore. Chicken Island, Ms. Mackenzie said it was called. Ivy's arms, legs, fingers—everything tingled. She was at a cabin; she was making a movie. They were doing the filming in just three days, one of them here, and they had a script, a shot list, and a schedule. There were only six days left until the deadline.

Ivy wiggled her fingers to warm them up and narrowed her eyes at the light.

"It's good," a voice said from behind her. Jacob came out from behind a clump of cedars. "I grabbed the camera when I woke up. *Early.* That couch was hard. And Kelly snores."

Ivy grinned. "Prairie does too."

"Anyway, I figured it wouldn't hurt to get some backup shots."

"You should get one of the kayak." Ms. Mackenzie's kayak lay tipped upside down a few feet away. Something about it was like Aunt Connie's umbrella. "I like the red of it against the sand."

Jacob went off with the camera; Ivy took a breath of the cold, tree-smelling air. She felt good. Bigger than herself.

Jacob finished shooting the kayak and moved down the beach. Ivy stayed by the boat. She wanted a minute alone before the day started.

By eleven they were filming scene twelve, *Approach to Kayak.* It wasn't going well. Tate, who was playing Heather, kept looking confident and strong as she limped up to the kayak on her crutch—an old one of Beryl's—when she needed to look scared.

"Cut!" Ivy called, loud for her. "I need uncertainty, Tate.

Fear. You're terrified of the water. You don't know if you can get in that boat and paddle across this lake, even if it's to meet your long-lost sister—"

They were going to film the scene where Heather's sister, who was being played by Prairie, scanned the sky for the seaplane that was coming to take her to Greenland to do research on polar bears. "Think about it. You've found out your sister is about to go off to do a big research project in the Arctic. If you don't catch her, you'll have no hope of tracking her down again for years because this project is going to take her so far into the wilderness. You have to do this. But you're scared. You're stuck. *Show* it. Can you?"

"Yes!" Tate snapped. Ivy smiled at her and Tate twisted her hair up around one hand. "I get it," she said, sighing. "I do."

"Okay. One more time and then we have to get out front. We've only got the bus for half an hour." Making a movie was more complicated than Ivy would ever have imagined. Ms. Mackenzie knew a man who organized a shuttle for senior citizens; he was bringing it by the cabin between runs, so they only had a few minutes to show the bus driver, being played by Kelly, encouraging Heather to continue her search for her sister.

You'll find her, Kelly-as-bus-driver had to say. *The address you've got there says Piney Lane—that's right on the lake. I can't get this bus up that road, but it's not far. You're almost there, don't give up.* But Heather's sister wouldn't be at the cabin on Piney

Lane when Heather limped up. The script called for her to be out on Chicken Island.

"We'll finish this, we'll do the bus thing, then break for lunch, then do the paddling scene—"

"But when do I come in?" Mrs. Grizzby asked anxiously, after they'd eaten the lunch that Dad Evers and Grammy had brought. They'd picked up Mrs. Grizzby too. Mom Evers and Daniel were at home because Mom Evers thought he was too young to stay through the whole day of filming.

Ivy hit Pause. She made herself smile calmly at Mrs. Grizzby, who was cast as the woman who'd kidnapped Heather and then followed her to Piney Lane. Only she and Ivy knew what she was going to say when she found Heather. Ivy had decided it was better to keep the cast in suspense about this. It'd make their reactions fresher. "Not yet. It's after Heather's already in the boat, on the water. The next scene. You yell at her to be careful, and then that other thing, remember?"

"But not now?"

"Not yet. I'll tell you when."

Mrs. Grizzby's smile was shaky. "I'm nervous! Isn't that silly?"

"You'll do great."

Mrs. Grizzby's real smile, the blinding one, flashed out then. "You think so?"

"I do." Ivy used her most positive voice, but the truth was, she didn't know. She didn't know about any of this. So far the movie seemed choppy, and the story a little bit silly. How likely was it that Heather would just happen to meet her sister's old professor when he visited her tutor at the estate one day, and that Heather looked so much like her sister the professor would recognize her? Or that the kidnapper would have kept track of what Heather's real family was doing all these years and know where the sister was at the exact time Heather set out to find her? Not very likely at all. Still, the movie was dear to Ivy. And no matter how it turned out, she knew she'd always love it for being her very first one. First but not last, she was determined.

Grammy patted Mrs. Grizzby's arm. She was playing her banjo for the sound track, so she'd be listed as a musician, but she should have another title too. Cast Manager, maybe. Mrs. Grizzby Manager.

Mrs. Grizzby gnawed at her lip and Ivy puffed out her cheeks. The next scene, where Mrs. Grizzby yelled out to Tate to be careful, and—this was the surprise—wished her luck in her quest, and Tate waved her paddle in farewell but kept moving steadily forward, was the last one in the movie. It wasn't the last one they'd shoot—shooting went according to light and locations and the props they could get—but Ivy would feel better when it was done. More certain. Like there was no turning back.

"Okay, everybody. Ready?"

Tate nodded. Prairie and Kelly, who were holding the kayak onshore, nodded. Jacob, who was holding the clapper boards that had the scene number chalked on before every take, on loan from the showcase in his grandparents' theater's lobby, nodded, and so did Beryl and Mrs. Grizzby and Ms. Mackenzie and Grammy and Dad Evers, even though all they were doing was watching. Ivy pointed at Jacob, Jacob snapped the clapper boards, and Ivy pressed Record.

An hour later, they were still at the beginning of the scene. They'd been at it so long that Beryl and Grammy and Dad Evers had headed off to the tiny general store in town to buy more coffee. Tate had finally managed to look uncertain for her approach to the kayak, but now that she needed to look graceful and sure, she didn't. She kept turning the boat in circles, splashing the water with the paddle.

"Cut!" Ivy called for the fifth time. "Tate—"

"I never drove a kayak before, I'm sorry! It's harder than it looks."

"Okay, I know. But we have a lot to get done. You have to talk to the bus driver, you have to deal with your supposed mother—"

"Now?" Mrs. Grizzby stepped forward. "Do I do my lines now?"

"Pretty soon." Ivy made herself smile calmly, though she didn't feel calm. The light was changing. "So, Tate, just do what Ms. Mackenzie said—"

"Dip smooth with the paddle." Ms. Mackenzie demonstrated with an invisible paddle. "Work with the water, not against it—"

"Right. Do that and kind of—*gaze*—forward. Think nervous but determined. Think, I can do this, even though everything I've ever been told tells me I can't. Think, I have a sister, she's just across that water—right? Got it?"

Tate nodded.

"Okay, kiddos," Ms. Mackenzie said. "You've got this. I just realized I should've gone with the others to town—I need to get the propane bottles refilled. C'mon, Inez, you come with me and let's leave them to it."

Ivy waited until they were climbing the steps off the beach. Then she said, "Okay. Scene thirteen, *Paddling*."

Tate sat up straight. She gave a solemn nod and Ivy hit Record again.

Just as she did, there was a screech of brakes. Ivy lowered the camera.

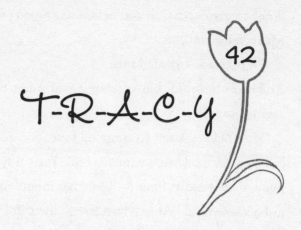

42

T-R-A-C-Y

The Mustang pulled in tight between two trees. Ivy's mother strode toward them. "Ivy! It took me forever to find you, what do you mean by taking off?"

"Mom." Pain blossomed in Ivy's head. "How did you know I was here?"

"Yeah, I'm glad to see you too. I'm doing okay, thanks for asking."

"Mom—"

"George dropped the charges, if that's what you're wondering." She made a *piff* sound through her teeth. "He was just inflating things, causing trouble, his eye's fine."

It was hard to know how to respond. Ivy settled on the most important part, that George's eye was okay. "Wow. That's good, it's great."

"I got out last night. Went to Family Services this morning. What a runaround. Can you believe they didn't want to tell me where you were?"

Yes. Ivy made a pained face.

"Finally they did, but of course you weren't there, so *that* was a goose chase."

"How did you know to come up here?"

Her mom made an unamused *heh.* "Yeah, fifty *miles* up." She pointed her head at Prairie. "I told her mom I had to see you."

Ivy's mom had lied to Mom Evers, then. Told her it was an emergency, something to make her sympathetic. Mom Evers probably even thought Ivy might want to see her mom. And maybe she did. "So—now what? You just go home?" asked Ivy.

"Oh, no. No way. I've had it with Kingston."

"You—you're moving? Just like that?"

"Just like that." Her mother snapped her fingers. "Nothing to wait for."

"But—where?"

"Detroit." *Dee*-troit, is how she said it.

"*Detroit?* Mom, that's in Michigan. You can't just move to Michigan."

"Says who?"

"But—why there?"

Ivy's mom jiggled her keys. The plastic cubes bounced and clacked. "It's what I decided, that's all. Come on if you're coming."

"What, right now? This minute?"

"Now or never."

Ivy gestured at the group behind her, as if maybe her mom hadn't noticed all these people were gathered at a lake fifty miles from home. "Mom, I'm in the middle of filming. Everybody's here, we only have the weekend—"

"I'm sorry, but this is real life, Ives. I don't have time to wait."

"But I have to do this. And we *live* here, Mom. *That's* real life. We have friends—"

Her mom made a *hmmph* noise. "What friends?"

Ivy held her hand out, palm up, toward everyone.

Her mother crossed her arms. "Okay. I'll give you the weekend, then we leave."

"But Jacob and I are starting a film club in the fall, we're going to meet at the library down the street from Beryl's, the librarian said we could. Plus Ms. Mackenzie's teaching my grade next year and she's my teacher again. She's the best—"

Her mom shook her head.

"And I want to do a movie about kids with careers. I already started. Prairie and Kelly are getting goats because you can make chee—"

Her mom snorted. "Kids with careers. Come on. Do you really think you're going to be some big movie director?"

Ivy felt ancient and exhausted. "I don't know. I have no idea. But I'm going to finish this, and I'm going to try." Each word weighed a hundred pounds.

"Bah," Ivy's mom said in a disgusted way.

Prairie muttered and Jacob took a step forward, but Ivy saw the fear in her mom's eyes. That undid her just when she felt mad enough to let her mother go back to Kingston and start packing by herself. She took a step forward. "Mom, listen. Why do you want to go all the way to Detroit? We don't know anybody there."

Ivy caught a shift in her mom's eyes.

"Mom. Do we know somebody there?"

"It's just, Dave said he might know of somebody looking for help—"

"*Dave.*"

"He said he's gonna head out there. He has a buddy who might get him work."

"*Dave?* Lindsey's boyfriend, Dave?"

"He came to see me while I was in jail. Apologized for Lindsey's nonsense and what all. They split up, you know."

"Mom, no. Not Dave, he's not—"

"He's not so bad. You'll see. He's looking for a place for us, something to get started—"

Ivy was nailed to the ground; a spike had been driven through her. When she could speak, she said, "I think you should stop running."

"Running! I'm not—"

"You should stop. It just makes everything worse."

Her mother's eyes went bright. "Ives—let's just go, okay?"

Her eyes were pleading. "We'll talk in the car." She joggled her keys.

Ivy stared at the key chain. Her mom had made it at a gas station. Doing that, making it, was private and innocent somehow, and—this was the worst part—hopeful. The beads between the cubes were pink and green and yellow and purple and so were the feathers dangling off the end. T-R-A-C-Y.

"Mom, listen—" Ivy said slowly.

Her mom had started talking at the same time. "This is a waste of time anyway. Like you can really make a movie."

Ivy's eyes snapped away from the key chain. "We *are* making one. We're in the middle of it, everybody's helping—"

Her mom's lips went thin. "I already told you, you try too hard. This whole thing—"

"It makes me feel close to my dad a little," Ivy said softly.

"Your *dad.* Please."

"He loved movies—"

"He didn't give a rat's—" Ivy's mother glanced at the group. "He didn't care about movies. Or you."

"Yes, he did!" Ivy cried. "He loved movies, and he loved me. He gave me that battleship game that last Christmas, he wrapped it himself—"

"It's all in the *past,* Ivy. Gone and over. For God's sake, grow *up.*"

Ivy stepped backward as the truth crashed into her. Her mom wasn't safe. Not for Ivy. She did have a good side. She might even, in a way, love Ivy. But she fought dirty. She was mean when she felt threatened, and almost everything made her feel that way. She would never put Ivy first. She'd hurt her as quick as swatting a fly, if hurting her was convenient. It wasn't news. It had been right in front of Ivy her whole life. She'd just tried hard not to see it.

After a moment her mother said, "C'mon, Ives. Don't look like that."

Ivy shook her head.

"I shouldn't have said that. Your dad loved you, 'course he did. And I guess he did like movies. It's just—I get mad." She tried out a smile, then let it fall away. She waited. Ivy didn't speak. Finally she said, gently, "Come on, get in the car. We'll talk on the way. Lots of time, on the road. We'll see Niagara Falls."

"No."

"Come *on*. Just get in the car."

"No. I'm staying here. I'm doing this."

Seconds passed. Ivy's mother turned and walked to the Mustang.

Ivy listened to the door screech open, watched her mom settle into the seat. Her mom put her hands on the steering wheel and looked over her shoulder, then backed away. The brakes squealed at the mouth of the drive, the engine roared as her mom hit the gas. Ivy listened until she couldn't hear the car winding down the road anymore.

Ivy shook her head. She turned to face her friends. After a moment, she smiled. It wasn't a real smile, but they'd understand. She lifted the camera.

"Okay," she said when she could. "Let's do this. Scene thirteen, *Paddling*."

43

Curtains

The house lights dimmed and the purple velvet curtains slid back. There was the flicker and clatter of an old-style movie reel—Ivy had loved that effect when Jacob showed it to her on his computer, which was a whole lot nicer than Aunt Connie's—and then the title appeared in cursive: *Heather Lake Investigates*. Ivy grabbed Prairie's hand and squeezed. There was her movie. Her clunky little movie, up on the screen.

They filled the sidewalk walking to the ice cream shop afterward: Ivy and Prairie and Jacob and Tate and Kelly; Mom and Dad Evers and Daniel and Grammy; Mrs. Grizzby and Beryl and Ms. Mackenzie and Ms. Mackenzie's date, the man with big ears, whose named turned out to be Thomas.

Ivy pulled on Prairie's arm to stop her for a second; everyone moved around them like water around rocks. "So you do really understand, right? Why I'm staying with Beryl?"

Prairie rolled her eyes. "Because you have a *turret*. Who can compete with a turret?"

"No—"

"No, I get it, I'm only teasing. I know you like town, and Ms. Mackenzie, and the film club and everything. I know you and Beryl get along, that she kind of—needs you, in a way. I mean, not *needs*—"

Ivy nodded. "She does, though. I mean, she doesn't, but she does. We kind of match. I fit there. I matter—"

Prairie started to say something, but Ivy knew what it was going to be. "Not that I don't matter to you guys, that's not what I mean. But I can *do* things for Beryl, and, I don't know—"

"I know," Prairie broke in. "I do."

Ivy puffed out her cheeks. She was glad they were back to understanding each other's garbled, unfinished sentences.

Prairie pulled Ivy's braid gently. "It's okay. I mean, I miss you, I do. But I understand."

"Thanks." Ivy tried to put everything she felt into her eyes.

Prairie grinned. "You're welcome. But they're leaving us behind." She grabbed Ivy's arm to drag her along faster.

Beryl clanged her spoon against her sundae glass to get everyone's attention once they were all sitting squeezed at one table in the ice cream shop's front window. "To Ivy!" she said, when everyone was looking at her.

"To Ivy!" everyone cried.

Ivy bit her lip; her grin got bigger anyway. Her movie hadn't placed or even won an honorable mention, but that didn't matter. She felt like the queen of the world. She pushed back her chair and stood up. She cleared her throat and looked at each person for a second. Then she said, quietly, "I couldn't have done it alone. So—to everyone."

"What did she say?" Mrs. Grizzby asked, frowning.

"Shout it out, Ivy," Grammy called.

Ivy took a deep breath. "To everyone!" she said, loud and clear.

This Train Ride

The train Ivy rode on rattled steadily down the track.

"Where do you think she is?" Ivy bounced the postcard from her mother on her palm. It had arrived in Beryl's mailbox a few days before, right at the end of September. There was a picture of Niagara Falls on the front. *It's a lot of water,* her mom had written. *Wouldn't want to go over it in a barrel. How'd that contest go?*

Grammy shook her head. "Maybe Detroit, like she told you."

Ivy peered at the postmark, but she already knew it was smudged and impossible to read. She tucked the card back into her sketchbook and looked out the window.

They were headed for the city. Grammy was taking her to a weekend filmmaking workshop for kids at the New York Public

Library, and it was just the two of them. Prairie had gone to the creamery with the 4-H club.

"I hope she's okay," Ivy said when the train passed Sing Sing prison, out on its rock in the Hudson River.

Grammy cleared her throat like she had a frog in it. Then she said, "Well, me too. Of course I do," She squeezed Ivy's hand.

A few more miles went by. A ray of sunlight fell in Ivy's eyes and she squinted. She smiled, her hand still held lightly in Grammy's.

It was strange to think how scared she'd been about the Everses knowing the bad things about her life with her mom. She'd been so angry at them, and so sure she had to hide the truth. She felt differently now. Something about making the movie, not giving up even when it seemed hopeless and dumb, and asking everyone to help—had changed her. That hole inside herself felt mended enough that she could see: the Everses hadn't looked down on her and pitied her. They'd only wanted to be part of her life, and to help.

"You'll hear from your mom again," Grammy said. "I really think you will. And who knows, maybe someday she'll get her act together. It *is* possible. She's not all bad, she couldn't be or there wouldn't be you, hanging around plaguing us with your interesting ideas and your movie projects and your flat-out blind determination to get the things done that you want to do." She poked Ivy's ribs in exactly the same way Prairie would've and Ivy giggled.

Grammy took her hand again and squeezed it, and Ivy went back to looking out the window. She might hear from her mom again, like Grammy said. Her mom might get her act more together. Right now though Ivy had something else to think about: this moment, this train ride, which was the best part of her day so far. She drew her braid over her shoulder and tugged at it and went back to her work, looking out at the world and taking it in.

Acknowledgments

For their contributions to Ivy's story, my thanks go to:

Kathleen Ernst, who listened at a crucial time.

Carly Miller, who thought I should draw my way into the story. Thanks for the pencils and sketchbook.

Joe and Lonnie Heywood, for always offering a comfortable lawn chair and good conversation.

Phil and Gavin Downs, who helped me with my pitching. Go, Boilermakers.

Terri Poliuto, First Reader. Thanks for demanding more chapters. (You know I was afraid not to comply.)

Robin Ryle, fellow writer and wonderful friend.

Mariann Airgood, Mark Airgood, Laura Bontrager, Maria Cantarero, Pamela Grath, Lisa Snapp, and Karen Wolf. More dear and valued readers. Thank you all for being in Ivy's corner.

John and Genie Hayner and Gary Michael. Thank you for being such great friends.

Joy Harris, my agent. Many *x*'s and *o*'s.

Nancy Paulsen, my editor. Thank you for your careful and patient attention to Ivy's story.

All at Nancy Paulsen Books who helped create this novel. Special thanks to the copy editor, Chandra Wohleber, whose comments were so apt, and to the designer of this perfect cover.

Matt and Peg Airgood, for their constant, loving interest in my endeavors.

Jean Guth, my mother-in-law, for her hospitality during an intense week of work on the manuscript. Thanks for understanding that I had to work, and for the Mint Klondike bars, too.

Our crew at the West Bay Diner. Their good cheer, hard work, and flexibility help make it possible for me to do two crazy jobs instead of just one.

Our customers, so many of whom are also dear friends and— hurrah!—book buyers.

The readers who were so enthusiastic in their response to *Prairie Evers*.

My parents, Henry and Anita Airgood. Both were voracious readers who filled our house with books. I couldn't have had better champions in life.

My husband, Eric Guth, who gets it.

Turn the page to see where Ivy
and Prairie's friendship began
in the companion novel—

ellen airgood

PRAIRIE EVERS

a story of friendship, growing up, and . . . chickens

THE OLD SHOE

Just exactly one year ago, right after midnight on New Year's Eve, my grammy told me, "Prairie, I have ushered in the new year with you, and that is all I can do. A body as old as me has only got so much time left. I've got to go home."

I stared at her, my hand hanging above the Monopoly board. I was the top hat and Grammy was the old shoe. Those are the pieces we always chose. I'd thought she seemed a little distracted— she let Reading Railroad go without a peep, and normally Grammy wouldn't let a railroad go for anything—but I'd put it down to the lateness of the hour. The big hand on the kitchen clock had already clicked past twelve with a little hop like it always does, and Mama and Daddy had tromped off to bed the very next instant. So it was just me and Grammy at the table, drinking RC Colas and playing Monopoly while outside the wind gnawed at the corners of the house and sent darts of cold in at the windows.

"You are now ten years of age. You're well grown and have your mama and daddy to look after you. I'm going back to North Carolina where I belong."

I could not believe what I was hearing. "But we just *got* here." I didn't feel that way really. We'd lived in New York State for three months so far and it already felt like a hundred years to me, but I had to try and talk her out of this idea any way I could.

"I'm sorry, child."

"You *can't* go. Where would you live?" Mama and Daddy sold our house on Peabody Mountain when we left North Carolina, and Grammy had always lived with us.

"I'll go to Vine's Cove. My roots are there, and here I'm withering like a tree yanked out of the earth."

I thought, You are my earth. How will I grow up any more without you?

Grammy read my thoughts plain. "You'll do all right. You have a good mama and daddy to help you along. But this life up north in New York State is not for me."

"It's not for me either," I declared. "I'll go with you."

I felt a great gust of relief at that idea. Of course it was the answer. Vine's Cove was the next closest thing to home, after Peabody Mountain. Grammy's brother, Great-Uncle Tecumseh Vine, lived there, and I liked him. He lived way back in the mountainy woods in the cabin he was born in, a little old shack made of pine logs and plank floors. It didn't look like much, but it had withstood the test of time for over one hundred years. That's what Grammy always said anyway.

"You can't do that, child. You have to stay here with your mama and daddy."

"Maybe Mama and Daddy will move back too, if we're there."

"Prairie, child, use your head. You know they've just got started here. You know they could never get this much land down home. It's only because your mama's folks passed on to their greater reward that they've got this now."

"Well, they may've gone on to their greater reward, but it hasn't turned out so good for me," I muttered. Then I ducked my head and hoped the Lord would not strike me down. Mama's folks had perished in a car accident, and it was very tragic. I knew that the way you know something in your head, but I always felt guilty I didn't feel it more in my heart. But the thing was, I never really knew them. They never got down to North Carolina and we never got up to New York State. Until now.

"Prairie, Prairie," Grammy said, sounding sorrowful.

"But I don't like it here. If you're going home, I'm going too."

"You can't."

"But—"

"You're young, you'll adjust. But my heart is broke, you see. I miss the smell of the mountains too much."

"It smells like mountains here." I couldn't believe I was defending this place, but it was true. It did smell like mountains here, a little different from home but still mountains—rocky and mossy and shadowy and good. If that was her reason for going, I couldn't let her get away with it.

Grammy gave me a sad, crinkly smile. "The plain fact is, I'm feeling old. My bones ache and my eyes are dim and my grinders have become few." She meant that she didn't have many of her own teeth left. She was grinning to take the sting out of all this, but it didn't work.

"Grammy."

"I'm not going to kick the bucket tomorrow. But I can't live the last of my life up here, so far from the sights and sounds I grew up with. I expected I could make this change but I cannot. My heart has turned toward home and I have got to follow. I'm sorry."

"But who will teach me?" I cried, my last stab at changing her mind.

"Your mama and daddy will finish out this school year." There was something odd about the way she said it, something unfinished that made me uneasy for a moment, but I didn't pay attention. My heart was so sad and surprised by what she was saying, I couldn't think straight.

Grammy frowned and smooched her lips out and frowned some more—it was to keep any tears from escaping, I knew—and then she rolled the dice and marched the old shoe down the board three spaces. She said, "Look there now, I've landed on your railroad. What is it that I owe you?"

I wanted to say "nothing" and shove away from the table and go to bed without another word. But I didn't. I stared at the board for a long time and then I said, "It is twenty-five dollars," as she well knew, being the railroad magnate that she was.

GOOD-BYE

A few days later we went to the bus station with Grammy and waved her away. I struggled mightily, but I couldn't keep from crying. My heart was cracking into a million pieces, and no matter how broken it got, it kept on breaking.

We went back to the house—I couldn't think of it as home yet—and Mama fixed lunch. I poked at my macaroni and cheese, which Mama makes all cheesy and bubbly and crunchy on top. Normally it's one of my favorite meals, but I didn't have any appetite. I went to my room and crawled under the covers.

Mama came and looked in on me after a while. "How are you holding up?"

"I hate it here. I want to go home."

Mama sat on the edge of my bed and patted my shoulder. "This was my room, you know," she said after a while. "I always liked that window that looks east. I liked to watch the sun rise. I felt like I was the first one seeing the world get born every day."

I sighed, but I liked knowing Mama and I felt the same about that window. The first thing I did every day back at home was look outside. I'd check on the weather and see the tangle of honeysuckle scrambling up the barn wall, the dark, quiet clump of rhododendron standing by the well house, the slender branches of the redbud tree etched against the mountainside. Here the view was different—there was a big hemlock tree giving the sky a sharp poke, an old chicken coop whose boards were as gray as a rainy day, a barn and some sheds and a meadow rolling slowly down the hill toward town—but it gave me the same good feeling to survey the world from up on high first thing.

"It's a good house," Mama said. "I hope you'll like it better here one day."

That made me feel like crying all over again. It sounded so final.

The house was a little old farmhouse with steep, narrow stairs to the second floor, where there were two bedrooms tucked up under the eaves, one small and the other one, where Grammy had slept, smaller yet. It had a shady screened-in porch along the front and a big kitchen in the back with a potbelly stove in the center of the room. Outside there was the chicken coop, a falling-down shed and a standing-up one, a little barn with a steep, pointy roof, and about a hundred acres of gardens and berry patches Mama and Daddy had all kinds of plans for. Well, not a hundred acres really, but plenty. There was a big grassy meadow on the east side of the property and a craggy rock cliff along the west. The farm sat at the end of a dead-end dirt road that ran alongside a chunk of the Shawangunk Mountains, and if you couldn't be at home in North Carolina, it was probably the next best thing. The house was homey and cozy even though the wind did whistle in at the windows some, and I had been getting just a little bit used to it all when Grammy took off and left me.

"It'll be too quiet up here now. Grammy and I always talked at night."

"I know you did."

"Every night we gave everything a good going over. What we saw on our walks and how the garden was doing and my lessons and everything. And she always read to me. It'll be too lonely. I won't be able to sleep."

Mama stroked a lock of my hair and said, "Well, Daddy and I can read to you if you want. And you can read to yourself, too."

"I know." It would be too mean to say it wouldn't be the same. I got along with my mama and daddy like bread and butter. But Grammy wasn't just my grammy. She was my teacher and my best friend too. For my whole life I'd been tagging after her, doing everything she did. We were always investigating. If we were outdoors, it was birds and trees and plants and bugs and the shape of clouds. Inside, it was the history of plumbing and where cocoa came from and how to make some crazy thing like eggs Benedict. Once, we even made our own marshmallows, or we tried anyway.

Grammy was always curious about things, and failing in an endeavor never got her down long. That was life, she said: noticing and trying. You didn't have to succeed as long as you put your back into the effort. Everything gave her an idea about something else—something she had read or seen—and we were constantly looking further into the matter. There were so many books in our house, we didn't even try to move them all north. Boxes and boxes got packed away and stowed in Great-Uncle Tecumseh's shed, which I knew fretted Grammy something awful. She feared the damp would get into them and the mice would chew their pages despite the mothballs she sprinkled all around. I was convinced that was half the reason she headed back home.

"It's like there's a ghost," I told Mama, but it wasn't like that really. It was like there was a great echoing emptiness that scared me more than any ghost ever could.

"I know. We'll miss her too." Mama kept on patting my shoulder, and after a while I felt a tiny bit less woeful.

"I'm hungry," I said.

"I could heat up some of the leftover macaroni and cheese."

I sighed. Then I said, "Okay." I followed Mama back down to the kitchen and sat in the rocker right close to the potbelly stove while she heated my lunch back up. I felt like an invalid who had only just begun to recover from a terrible flu.